SPELUNKING SPECULATION

A MAGICAL MANE MYSTERY

STELLA BIXBY

FERRY TAIL PUBLISHING LLC

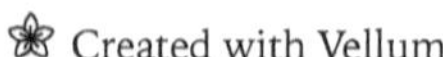 Created with Vellum

For Keri.

I am so thankful Mom and Dad didn't stop with me. Little did I know—when I asked when we could take you back to the hospital —that you'd become my best friend. I love you and am so proud of you.

CAST OF CHARACTERS

Ellie - Main Character

Penelope - Ellie's Pet Pig

Mona - Ellie's VW Microbus

Esme - Ellie's Grandmother

Emily - Ellie's Mother

Xander - Hunky Warlock

Jake - Police Chief/Emily's High School Sweetheart

Bex - Ellie's Best Friend/Works at Katie's Café

Deb - Local Police Officer/Bex's Sister

Katie - Married to Earl/Own's Katie's Café & Theater

Melody - Katie & Earl's Daughter/Hollywood Actress

Fran - Coupled with Amy/Own's Fran's Fabric & Feed

Amy - Coupled with Fran/Own's Amy's Antiques

Nancy - Married to Hank/Own's Nancy's Nails

Bonnie - Own's Helen's Hardware & Development Company

Renée - Widowed/Grand Witch of the States

Lucy - Ellie's Friend/Misty & Melly May's Grandmother

Misty - Local Police Officer/Melly May's Twin

Melly May - Misty's Twin

Trisha - Park Volunteer/Works at B&B

Belinda - Own's Belinda's B&B/Laura's Mom

Laura - Bex's Friend

Bernardo - Spicy Warlock/Xander's Cousin

Georgia - Jake's Fiancée

A Note to readers: Thank you so much for reading *Spelunking Speculation*!

If you haven't already, check out the free short story *Argentina Abduction* that takes place before this book begins! You can find it at:

www.stellabixby.com/AA

Happy Reading!

L ight peeked through the windows of the barn as we took our last deep breaths.

"You all did wonderfully today," I said to the smiles around the room. Slowly, the morning workout class had grown from being a handful of women to a whole gaggle of them. As a result, it became increasingly challenging to incorporate the exercises and make them challenging for all ages.

"Soon, we'll be able to take our exercises outside." I couldn't wait for that day. Finally, the chill seemed to have left the air, and the snow was almost gone. I'd almost made it through my first Iowa winter.

"Will we transition into running?" Renée asked, wiping the sweat from her wrinkled forehead. She had short white hair, kind eyes, and an outfit so bright I almost had to squint looking at her.

"We'll either run or walk," I said. "I like to push everyone to do their best, but I don't want anyone to get hurt."

"You youngins can run all you like, but my knees won't take all the pounding," Renée said.

Fran and Nancy nodded along with her as Katie and Bonnie handed out post-workout coffees.

"Thank you." I took mine and sipped the liquid energy. The caffeine seemed to seep directly into my bloodstream and up to my scalp.

"Any word on that ring those hikers found this morning?" Katie asked Deb. Deb was one of the local police officers and usually relatively tight-lipped when it came to her job. This didn't stop Katie—or any of the women—from asking.

"Nothing yet," Deb said.

"It has to belong to Melly May," Amy said, pushing her bright green-dyed hair over her shoulder. "The finger they found years back is the same one she would have worn it on."

I nearly choked on my coffee. "I'm sorry, I thought you said finger."

"I did." Amy smiled.

"A few years back, a woman named Melly May went missing. All we found of her was her finger," Deb said. "With no additional evidence and with the location and condition of the finger, we assumed she'd gone over the falls."

"Those falls are dangerous," Katie said. "So many people have died up there. I've heard it's haunted, but I'm too chicken to see for myself."

"Where are these falls?" I asked. Most of the surrounding area was cornfields and pig farms.

"They're in the state park," Amy said, "with the caves and the cliffs."

"And now someone found a ring?" I asked.

"Yes," Deb said slowly, trying not to give anything away. "But we haven't gotten confirmation that it was Melly May's yet."

"I'd think Misty could confirm it, couldn't she?" Katie asked.

Deb didn't reply.

"Remind me who Misty is?" The name was familiar, but I couldn't place her.

"She's one of the officers," Deb said. "You met her on the last case."

"Lucy's granddaughter?" I asked, doing a mental head slap. Of course, Lucy had talked about her several times.

Deb nodded.

"Lucy never mentioned one of her granddaughters

died," I said. While on the last case, Misty had asked me to visit her grandmother to help her with her shoe-tying—my business being recreational therapy. Since then, I'd spent more time than necessary at Sunny Meadows—the assisted living home—chatting and doing puzzles with Lucy.

"Misty and Melly May were twins," Katie said. "I'm sure it's simply too hard to speak of."

The other women nodded.

It made sense, but still. I thought Lucy and I were closer than that. I'd even talked to her about my time in foster homes.

"What would it change if Misty did identify the ring as being Melly May's?" I asked.

Deb sucked in a breath. She wasn't supposed to talk about this, but it would be public knowledge by the end of the day anyway, with the way word spread in our little town. "The family always said they didn't think it was possible Melly May would take her own life."

"Meaning this could be new evidence in a potential murder case?" I asked.

"Or abduction. Or runaway." Deb shrugged. "It could be several things."

"Melly May wouldn't have run away," Fran said. "She worked at my store for a few years. She loved it here. Misty was the one who wanted out of town."

"Either way," Deb said. "It's just a ring. And even if it is Melly May's, it doesn't necessarily change anything."

I saw wisps of my hair changing from its usual white to a shade of burgundy from the corner of my eye.

"Uh—" Katie pointed at my head.

"Nope," Deb said. "We can't go off the color of her hair. We did that way too much with Esme."

Esme—my grandmother—had the same magical hair as both me and my mother, Emily. Esme had died before I'd been able to meet her. Emily was presumably still alive, but she'd dropped me off at a fire station when I was a newborn. No one—including Esme—had even known I existed.

"It may not be concrete evidence," I said. "But my hair isn't usually wrong. Sometimes, it's misinterpreted, but not wrong."

Katie looked expectantly at Deb.

"Fine," Deb said. "I'll look into it more closely when I get to work. But I don't think it'll change anything. What can one ring do?"

"You're engaged?" I gaped at the massive diamond on Georgia Barnette's hand as Jake proudly showed off his fiancée.

I was standing in the middle of Katie's Café, right in the middle of pouring a steaming hot cup of coffee. It took everything in me to steady my hand and not let the scalding liquid run over the rim of the mug and onto the table.

"Isn't it beautiful?" Georgia asked. "It was his grandmother's."

A knot twisted in my stomach. Jake had dated my mother before she'd gone missing. When I'd first moved to town, I thought he could be my father. But he'd dispelled that notion rather quickly. Even so, he'd never given up on finding Emily. Until Georgia came around and took all of his attention.

"It's great," I choked out. "Congratulations. I'll—uh—go get your coffee and pancakes."

I was covering for Bex at the café this morning. She'd gone on vacation with her friend, Laura.

The café wasn't crowded, but it felt unusually stuffy.

"Okay, spill," a voice said behind me.

I turned to find Jake with his hands on his hips and his investigator face on. He was the local police chief.

"What do you mean? The coffee?" I laughed at my stupid joke. Bex would have thought it was hilarious, but Jake saw right through me.

"Not the coffee," he said. "The ring? Georgia? You didn't seem very excited for me, and I think I know why."

"You do?"

"You think that just because I'm getting married, I'll stop looking for Emily."

He was partially right. "I guess."

"Don't worry, Ellie," he said. "I'll never stop looking for her."

I wanted to scream at him. What happened when he found her? What if she still wanted to be with him? We could be a family. He could be my dad, even if we weren't related by blood.

But that wasn't fair. Not to him. He'd spent over twenty years waiting for her to come back. He deserved to be happy.

I did my best to look relieved. "I'm glad to hear that."

He smiled and squeezed my shoulder, then turned and walked back to Georgia, who beamed at him.

Ever since Xander—one of my magical friends—told me Georgia was his cousin—and a witch—I'd been skeptical of her. But she'd done so much good for the town in her short amount of time here.

She was a freelance journalist and wrote an article about the delicious, crispy-edged pancakes for which Katie's Café was famous. The café's business had been booming ever since—a big deal in the cold Iowa winter.

I tried not to think about if and when Emily came back to town. Heck, she could have moved on herself. But I knew deep inside that wasn't the case. I'd recently tried to use my magic to trace her and had gotten the feeling she was being held somewhere against her will. Possibly in a train tunnel.

Xander didn't like that I was using my magic to find her. He said it was dangerous and could hurt me. But all it ever did was make me tired.

When I got home later that day, I decided to see if the mural in the back of my barn had changed. Penelope met me in the driveway after I parked Mona—my VW Microbus—and oinked happily when I opened the door to the barn.

She had her own piggy door to get in and out of the house, but I refused to put one in the barn. I didn't need muddy little piggy prints all over my studio.

I followed her to the back and pulled the curtain to the side to reveal the same dreary painting as it had been for months—a train tunnel with a pinpoint of light at the end.

The light sometimes seemed to have faded, but that could have just been my imagination.

Before it had changed to this, it had always been a mural of the farm Esme left me. Sometimes there were people in the mural, but it was always some iteration of the barn, house, and corn. And in the lower right-hand corner was a signature I could probably recreate with my eyes closed—*Emily Vanderwick*.

How the mural changed when Emily was nowhere to be found was beyond me. There was a lot about magic I still hadn't figured out.

But one thing I was getting better at was knowing when someone was sneaking up behind me. "Xander, what are you doing here?"

I sensed his smile before I even turned around. "You're getting good at that."

"I wouldn't have to be if people wouldn't sneak up on me so often."

I turned to see one of the most handsome men I'd ever met. He had green eyes, long brown hair pulled up into a bun on top of his head, and wore his typical leather attire. He was a bad boy in warlock form . . . and he was dating someone else.

"Any changes to the mural?" He bent down and picked Penelope up. She wiggled her nose against his cheek.

"Nope." I tore my eyes off their adorableness to look back at the dark mural in front of me. "I'm starting to worry. I haven't been able to do the tracking spell for Emily again. It's like every time I try, my magic is blocked."

A pit settled in my stomach at this thought. What if Emily was blocking me? What if she didn't want to be found?

"How often have you tried?" Xander asked, worry laced through his words.

"A couple times a day at most. But I've tried at all different times of the day and night and always come across the same thing." I sucked in a breath. "Do you think she might be blocking me?"

I wanted him to tell me I was being crazy. That there was no way a mother would block her child from finding her. But Xander didn't lie to me. He might not have told me everything—or really anything, especially when it came to his personal life—but he never lied.

"It's a possibility," he said as gently as he could. He handed Penelope to me, and she snuggled into my arms, trying to make me feel better.

"But it's not the only possibility," Xander added.

"What are the other possibilities?"

Xander scrunched up his nose and looked away. He'd regretted saying that.

"It's okay. I can handle it."

"If something is blocking your magic, it has to be something magical. Or someone magical."

"Right," I said. "So it's probably whoever has my mother captive."

"That's a possibility." Xander's voice was near a whisper. He wrapped an arm around my shoulders, and Penelope's head shot up to look at him.

We both laughed.

For some reason, Penelope didn't like it when Xander and I got close. She really didn't like it when we kissed. Not that we'd done that more than once several months ago, but I would guess Xander still had a scar from her bite.

"Have you heard from the Grand Witch lately?"

"From Renée?" I asked. It was still weird thinking of her as the Grand Witch of the States. When we were in

Argentina, I'd discovered this bit of information after being led on a wild goose chase. It had been stressful, but the memory made me smile.

"You really shouldn't call her by her proper name." Xander's words pulled me from my memory.

"She was my friend before I knew she was the Grand Witch," I said. "Plus, she never corrects me when I call her Renée."

Xander sighed.

"But yes, I've heard from her," I said. "She was at my class this morning."

"Have you asked for her help with finding Emily?"

I blushed. "No."

"Why not?"

"Because it's strange," I said. "I don't want to burden her with my stuff. I'm sure she's busy enough with all her Grand Witch business."

"If anyone could help you, she could."

He was right. And I wanted to find my mother. But every time I almost got the nerve up to ask about it, the conversation would change, or I'd lose my train of thought.

"How about we go see her right now?" Xander asked.

I shook my head. "This is something I have to do alone."

When I called Renée's cell, she picked up on the second ring.

"How's my favorite witch?" she asked. Her bubbly voice instantly put a smile on my face.

"I'm doing well, thanks," I said. "How are you?"

"I'm wonderful. Just about ready to head out to visit an old friend."

"Oh," I said. "I'm sorry. I can call you another time."

"Nonsense," she said. "In fact, if you're free, why don't you come with me?"

I agreed to meet her at her house as soon as I changed out of my work clothes.

Her house was massive—much larger than typical Iowa farmhouses. She and her recently deceased husband had built it with what I thought was money from a blackmail business he had on the side. But now, I considered their wealth might have had more to do with Renée's position in the magical world.

She backed her car out of the garage as I put Mona in park.

I hopped in the passenger seat and was met with a warm smile.

"You look flustered," she said. "Is everything okay?"

I figured I might as well get it out in the open before I lost my nerve. "I wanted to know if you could help me—"

Her phone buzzed in the storage compartment between us.

"I'm so sorry, I have to take this," she said. She pressed a button in her left ear and said, "Hello?"

I couldn't hear what the person on the other end was saying, but it didn't seem good based on Renée's expression. "Right. Yes, I understand. I'll take care of it."

She hung up and hit the gas. Thankfully, there wasn't ice on the roads anymore, or we would have ended up in a ditch.

"Is everything okay?" I asked.

She smiled, but it wasn't the same genuine smile she gave me when I got in the car. "Everything's fine. We just have to make a quick pit stop before we head out to see my friend."

The car slid on the gravel road as we made our way to the highway that would lead us to town.

I considered bringing up Emily, but by the look on Renée's face, it didn't seem to be the right time.

When we pulled into the police station, I glanced over at Renée. "The police station?"

"I just have to pick something up," she said. "I'll be quick."

She hurried inside, leaving the car running. The air outside was warm enough. I didn't need the heat or air conditioning, but it was nice that she'd left me with the ability to at least roll down my window.

The breeze carried the smell of spring into the car as the window inched down. A lawnmower hummed in the distance. I closed my eyes and smiled. I loved the spring.

"All done," Renée said, slipping back into the car. She had nothing in her hand, and I wasn't brave enough to ask what she'd picked up.

Usually, I would have, but Xander questioning me about calling her Renée had gotten to me. Maybe I wasn't being respectful enough. I knew little about the magical world, but I'd surely need to be more serious when I was around the Grand Witch.

"Okay, what's the deal?" Renée said, turning out of town.

"What do you mean?" I shifted in my seat.

"You're acting strangely today."

"Am I?"

"Come on, tell me."

I took a deep breath. "Xander told me this morning I shouldn't call you Renée."

She thought about this for a moment as my insides churned. "So now you feel weird around me, is that it? Because I have more authority in the magical community than you?"

I nodded.

"I can understand his position," she said. "He grew up with magical rules, surrounded by magic. You did not."

"But shouldn't I learn? I don't even know the rules. What if I break them?"

"*If* you break them?" She laughed.

"Have I broken them?" Dread crept up my spine. I didn't like breaking the rules.

"Don't worry," she said. "It is only to be expected. Why do you think they assigned me to Cliff Haven in the first place?"

She was not making me feel any better. "You had to come here because of me?"

"You're a special witch, Ellie." She turned down a gravel road with which I was incredibly familiar. "I wouldn't be here unless it was important. But don't worry so much. Part of what makes you special is that you didn't grow up in the magical world. You're experiencing every-thing for the first time." She put the car in park when we were in front of the large main house. "And don't you dare call me the Grand Witch. I was your friend first and fore-most and will continue to be your friend, above all. To you, I am Renée."

Relief replaced the dread, and I could feel my hair changing. At one point, Renée had said she wanted color-changing hair. This was before I could sometimes sense when other magical people were around me. She must have found it so amusing that I had no idea she was magical herself. Especially when she said she wished she was a witch.

"Shall we go inside?" Renée asked.

4

The woman at the front desk recognized both Renée and me when we walked in. "Hello, how can I help you?"

I'd been to Sunny Meadows several times to visit Lucy, but I didn't know Renée had friends here as well.

"We'd like to see Lucy Blake, please," Renée said and winked at me.

"Right this way," the woman said. "And how has your day been, Grand Witch?"

I stopped in my tracks. Did she just call Renée Grand Witch? As in, she knew Renée was a witch? Did she know I was too? Was she?

I searched for the edges of magic and was overwhelmed by what I found. Not only was the front desk woman a witch, but the entire place was magical.

"Ellie, are you coming?" Renée asked, glancing back at me.

I hurried to catch up, looking around as if everything was new. And it looked new. At least newer. Before I could see the magic, it seemed like just an old farmhouse, but now it was downright sparkly. Magic hummed from every wall, every door. Even the ceiling seemed to glisten. It was breathtaking.

"Here we are," Renée said. "Thank you."

The woman did a slight bow and left back down the hall.

"This place is magical."

"I'm glad you finally saw it," Renée said. "Lucy told me you've been coming to visit her at Misty's request."

"Is she a witch?"

"Everyone in this facility is a witch or warlock. This is assisted living for the magical."

"I wouldn't think the magical would need assistance."

"You helped me with my strength," Renée said. "And Lucy with tying her shoes. Everyone needs help once in a while."

This reminded me of talking to her about my mom, but before I could, she knocked on the door. Lucy opened it as if she had been waiting.

"Good day, Renée," Lucy said.

"It's always a good day when I get to see you," Renée said, hugging Lucy. "And I brought Ellie along with me."

"What a treat," Lucy said, clapping her wrinkled hands together. "Two of my favorite people in one visit."

"I'm afraid this visit will be less of a treat than usual," Renée said. "Can we come in?"

Lucy opened the door wider, and the room transformed. What had before been a simple, tidy room was now more of a luxurious suite. "Let's sit at the table."

Before, there hadn't been a table. The room had been

so small without magic that when we did the shoe-tying sessions, we'd always had a hard time finding a place where we could both fit.

"Isn't magic wonderful?" Renée asked.

Lucy frowned but said nothing.

We sat around the table. Renée pulled something from the pocket of her jeans. "I believe this was Melly May's."

Lucy took the ring out of Renée's hand, and her eyes glazed with tears. "I'd heard rumors, but I didn't want to assume."

"Misty identified it this morning," Renée said.

Misty was Lucy's granddaughter, and Lucy was a witch. That meant Misty would be a witch as well. And her sister—the one who had likely been wearing this ring —had been one too. How had I not seen it before with Misty or Lucy? It had been so obvious in Argentina, but my magical abilities had been stifled since I'd been back in Iowa.

"Melly May was wearing it the day she went missing," Lucy said. "The finger they found was the finger she would have been wearing it on. It only makes sense they'd find the ring, eventually."

"But this many years later?" Renée asked.

"I can't go down that route again," Lucy said. "It cost me everything and landed me here."

"This place isn't so bad," Renée said.

"It's for the best. And you're right. It's not bad. Especially when friends come to visit." She winked at me.

I smiled. "Can I ask you a question?"

"Of course," Lucy said.

"Why didn't Misty bring you the ring?" I asked.

"Misty and I have . . . grown apart," Lucy said. "Since her sister went missing, she has wanted little to do with me. Which serves me right after all the trouble I put her through as a child. I figured she could handle it—thought it would make her better in the long run. Which, maybe it has. Look at her now. She's a police officer."

"Were the girls identical?" I asked.

"In most ways, yes," Lucy said, a shadow crossing her face. "Though I could typically tell them apart. Especially after the incident with the dog. Misty was never the same after that dog bit her."

"Did she have scars?" I asked, not remembering any visible scars from when I'd met her.

"Not to her body, but to her magic," Lucy said. "It seemed to strengthen her in some ways, but she was never the same around animals again."

It was a good thing there wasn't a K-9 unit in our police department.

"Do you think Melly May is alive?" Renée asked.

Lucy sucked in a breath, then finally said. "I don't know."

"Is there any way to use magic to find out?" I asked.

Renée peeked over at me with a grin.

"Only a witch with tracking abilities would know for sure," Lucy said. "And the last one of those was Esme."

I nodded. "Did she ever try for you?"

"She did," Lucy said. "But her health was declining. You see, many factors affect magic. In your case, you haven't used your magic your entire life, so you have to build up those skills. For me, I haven't used mine in years. If I wanted to, I'd have to rebuild my skills. And when your health isn't at its best, your magic doesn't work its best either."

Getting information about magic felt like a warm mug of cocoa on a chilly spring morning. Xander had been so closed-off when it came to teaching me anything.

"I think I might have the same magical abilities that Esme did," I said.

Renée leaned forward. "And that's exactly why I brought you here."

"They don't call you the Grand Witch for nothing," Lucy said.

"So even the Grand Witch doesn't have tracking magic?" I asked.

"We are all blessed with different kinds of magic," Renée said. "It's what makes us unique and reliant upon one another. If we could all do the same things, we wouldn't need anyone else."

"Do you think she'll be able to locate Melly May?" Lucy asked, her voice quiet as she turned the ring over in her hand.

"I think it's worth a shot," Renée said. "As long as Ellie's willing?"

"Of course I am," I said. "I'd love to help you find her."

"I have to forewarn you," Renée said. "If she hasn't used her magic all these years or if she is no longer living, you won't be able to sense her presence."

"So I can only locate magical people who are alive?" I asked.

"As far as we know, that's correct," Renée said. "Now, take the ring."

Lucy handed me the ring, and the moment it touched my palm, it warmed. "I can feel its magic."

"Good," Renée said. "Now focus."

I closed my eyes and thought about Melly May—the woman who had last worn the ring. Instantly, my mind rushed over the hills and to a treed area.

"The caves," I said. "She's in the caves."

5

I could see it clear as day. The opening of the cave was deep in the forest, down a narrow path. Melly May was there, and she was scared.

"Can you see her?" Lucy asked, her voice bordering on excitement.

"I can't see Melly May herself," I said, keeping my eyes closed. "But I can sense her magic and her fear."

"Does that mean she's alive?" Lucy asked.

"Why is she afraid?" Renée asked, ignoring Lucy's question.

"I don't know why, but I can feel the fear radiating off of her, out of the caves and down the path. It's like a streak of red leading me right to her."

"You could find her?" Lucy asked, resting her hand on my arm.

I opened my eyes to see a woman who had hoped for this moment for years.

"I think so," I said.

"Then we'll leave tonight," Renée said.

"Us?" I asked. "Like you and me?" The thought of Renée walking around those trails was ridiculous.

"You're not going without me," Lucy said.

"No, no, no," I said. "I can't take you. It looks like it's a hard path. I've worked with both of you enough to know that your strength and stamina aren't up to such a hike."

"Can you use your magic to boost us?" Lucy asked. "Like you did when you helped me with my shoes."

I'd often wondered if people got better because of my touch or if I was just that good at my job. I liked to think it was a bit of both.

"No," Renée said. "If she uses her magic to boost us, it'll deplete her reserves. She has the strength to get back there without her magic, but she'll need her magic to track Melly May. Is there anyone else who might go with you?"

"Bex and Laura are gone," I said. "Deb probably has to work. I could ask Jake."

"The police chief?" Renée asked.

I nodded.

"He was talking about his vacation this morning when I got the ring. It looked like he was getting ready to head out," Renée said.

He and Georgia were probably going to celebrate their engagement. Ugh.

"We shouldn't involve the police just yet," Lucy said. "I don't want to get Misty's hopes up just to let her down."

"What about Xander? He'd probably love to go with you." Renée winked.

"He's dating Laura," I said. "I don't think she'd love

the idea of him going hiking with me alone while she's out of town."

"This is practically a business trip," Lucy said. "And isn't it his business to—"

"Take care of his magical friends," Renée said, finishing her sentence. "Yes. It is. And if the Grand Witch tells him to go, he'll have no choice."

It wasn't exactly the best feeling to know a man had to be ordered to go somewhere with me. "How about I just ask him first?"

Renée shrugged. "But if he says no, I'll compel him to change his mind."

"As in mind manipulation?" I gaped at her.

Renée and Lucy both started laughing.

Apparently, that was a no.

"We can't use our magic to mess with someone's thoughts," Renée said. "It's not only against magical law. It's also impossible."

"Can you imagine what kind of damage that would do?" Lucy said with a shudder. "A person's thoughts should always be their own."

"Let's get you home so you can get ready." Renée stood. "Can we take the ring? Ellie might need it to track Melly May."

"Feel free," Lucy said.

When we were back in the car, I decided to ask Renée what I'd been planning on asking her from the get-go. "You said before that only certain witches could track other witches, right?"

"Yes." Renée snuck a peek over at me. "I wondered when

we'd be having this conversation. After you tracked me, I figured it was just a matter of time before you tried to track your mother. But I'm guessing you haven't had any luck."

I swallowed, trying to clear the lump in my throat. "I've had a bit of luck, but nothing like I had with Melly May. Do you think that's because my mother doesn't want to be found?"

Renée considered this for a moment. "That could be one reason you're having trouble."

"What would another reason be?"

"She could be too far away, or not using her magic," Renée said. "Though that would be quite the waste with a Vanderwick."

"Do you think someone might have her held captive?" I asked. "One of my cousins was in town a few months ago and—"

"I know all about Harriet's thoughts on the matter."

"And you think they're wrong?"

"Not specifically wrong," Renée said. "But I don't think they're necessarily correct either. Nothing she's given me has definitively pointed me in that direction."

"Do you handle magical police matters?" I asked.

"I am the Grand Witch of the States," Renée said. "I'm kind of like the President. I rarely get bogged down in the details."

"Except with Melly May?"

"Lucy and I have been friends for many years. When Melly May went missing, Lucy and Misty were devastated. Now, they hardly ever speak to one another."

"But when I spoke to Misty, she seemed very fond of

her grandmother. She's the one who asked me to help Lucy with her shoes."

"I'm sure she loves her grandmother, but Melly May was Lucy's favorite growing up. She was the high achiever, while Misty was the troublemaker. I suspect that's why she went into non-magical law enforcement and turned away from her magic altogether."

"I can't imagine what it's like to have a sibling," I said. "Not a real one, anyway. With the foster families, I was usually the odd one out."

"We've never talked about it, but I'd like to ask you not to hold too much against your mother. She lived in the shadow of one of the greatest witches of our time. Esme was a force to be reckoned with, and Emily was a free spirit. They had a good relationship, but I always thought Esme was too hard on her."

"I guess if I ever get to meet Emily, I'll be able to decide how I feel," I said. "But for now, I'm giving her the benefit of the doubt."

"Good," Renée said, pulling into her driveway. "Now, go home and get packed. Call Xander and bring Penelope to stay here."

The authority in her voice gave me a sense of purpose. I might not have been able to find my mother, but maybe I could use my magic to help someone else find their loved one.

6

When I got home, I started digging in the back of Esme's old closet to see if she had any hiking equipment. I hit the jackpot in one of the last boxes—backpacks, hiking boots, head-lamps, and even walking sticks.

Penelope gave me a funny look when I emerged from the closet holding all the items. "I'm going hiking to look for someone."

She oinked as if she was worried for me.

"It's okay," I said. "I'll ask Xander to go, and you'll stay with Renée. She's the Grand Witch of the States, so I'm sure she'll take very good care of you."

Penelope didn't look convinced.

I picked up my cell phone and tapped on Xander's contact.

"Hello?" Xander sounded like he had been sleeping.

"Did I wake you?" I asked, glancing at my watch. It was getting late.

"Yeah," he said. "But that's okay. What's up?"

"I have a favor to ask."

He grunted.

"I tracked Melly May—a missing witch—to the caves in the state park. I'm heading out there tonight to see if I can find her. Would you have time to go with me?"

"You're heading out tonight?" Xander said. "Why not wait until morning?"

"It's a rather urgent matter," I said. "She seemed afraid."

"You tracked her and felt her emotions?"

"I guess so," I said. "Renée wants me to go right away."

"Why didn't you lead with that?" I could hear him getting things together in the background. "I'm guessing I have no choice in the matter."

I hated that he seemed irritated.

"You have a choice," I said. "If you don't want to go, you don't have to go."

"I'll be there in a half-hour." He disconnected the call.

"That went well," I said to Penelope.

She nudged me with her snout. I sank to the floor and pulled her into my lap, snuggling her into me. "I'll miss you."

Her snout wiggled against my cheek, her little whiskers tickling my face.

"I love you too."

Xander and I drove in silence to Renée's house. Penelope sat in Xander's lap while I maneuvered Mona into the driveway. Penelope trotted up the steps ahead of us.

"Did I mess up your plans for the evening?" I asked Xander, my voice hushed.

"I didn't have any plans," he said.

"Then why are you so quiet?"

"I don't like being told what to do," he said. "But that's a me issue, not a you issue."

"If you don't want to go, you don't have to."

"Oh yes, he does," Renée said. I hadn't realized she'd opened the door.

Xander shot me a look.

Penelope bowed slightly at Renée's. Apparently, even she knew Renée was the Grand Witch.

"I'd invite you in, but you have a lot of ground to make up." Renée picked Penelope up off my lap. "Don't worry about us. We'll have a great time."

I kissed Penelope on the head. "Thanks for watching her."

"Be safe," Renée said.

When Xander and I were headed back down the driveway, my phone chimed.

I picked it up to see a text from Bernardo—Xander's cousin.

I hope you're doing well. I miss your moves.

"What's that smile about?" Xander asked.

I hadn't realized I was smiling. "It's nothing."

"Who's the text from?"

"Bernardo."

Xander shook his head but smiled. "What's he got to say?"

"Nothing much." I clicked the phone off and turned the key in the ignition.

"Oh," Xander said, his smile going back into a frown.

"What's the oh about?"

"I didn't realize the two of you texted, that's all."

"He's a good guy," I said. "We had fun when I was in Argentina."

Xander mumbled, "I bet you did."

"What is that supposed to mean?" I turned down the gravel road toward the state park.

"Bernardo is famous for showing the ladies a good time."

Whether he was just trying to get under my skin or telling the truth, I wasn't sure, but it stung nonetheless.

My phone pinged again, but I didn't want to pick it up while I was driving.

Xander glanced over and then turned and looked out the window.

Why did he care so much that I was texting his cousin? He was dating Laura. He didn't get a say in my love life.

The cornfields were still barren but getting ready for planting. As soon as the chance for a below-freezing night was gone, the farmers would be in the fields.

But where was the state park? I didn't even see any trees.

Then, when I came over a hill, it was like a portal to another realm. Not that other realms existed. At least, not ones I was aware of. I didn't know magic existed a year ago.

Either way, the fields turned into trees, the gravel road was paved, and a sense of anticipation stole over me. This was where we'd find Melly May.

Xander unloaded the backpacks and other items while I checked my message from Bernardo.

I'd like to visit you if you're up for it.

I quickly texted back.

Anytime! :)

"Let's get this over with so we can go back to our warm beds." Xander handed me my backpack and headlamp while watching me slide my phone into the back pocket of my jeans.

I took the ring out of my front pocket and turned it over in my hand. I didn't want to wear it in case it would lose its tracking abilities. As my eyes closed, the red trail appeared once more. This would be a piece of cake.

7

The trail we needed to take was muddy, held together only by the root system of the trees.

We headed off at a quick pace, only slowing when we had to brace ourselves on a branch or rock to get up or down a section of path.

"How far back is she?" Xander asked. "And why didn't Renée tell you to call the police? What if someone has her captive back here?"

"I don't know how far back," I said. "But we may have to sleep out here. I brought a tent. And about Renée, she and Lucy thought it might be too traumatic for Misty to deal with in case my magic isn't telling the truth."

"They think your magic could mislead you?"

"Or maybe they didn't want her to be the one to find her sister if her sister is dead by the time we get there."

"Great, so send us out to confront the trails and snakes and caves and murderers."

"I take it you're not much of an outdoorsman."

"I like the outdoors just fine. In the day. When I can see where I'm going and what I'm stepping on."

I stifled the giggle that wanted to burst from my chest. I'd grown up in Colorado and often went camping with my foster families or by myself after I was on my own. Being outside in the dark was one of my absolute favorite things to do.

"Be careful there," I said, pointing. "That looks like it might be an embankment."

Xander steered further from the edge than necessary. "How did you see that? I never would have seen that. I could have fallen right off there."

I stopped and turned to face him.

He winced as my headlamp shined right in his eyes.

"Sorry." I turned it off and put my hands on his arms. Instantly, I felt pure panic rising through my palms. He was genuinely scared.

I took a deep breath and tried to focus calming energy back into him. "It'll be okay. I've spent much of my adult life sleeping outside. If you really want to go back, we can stay in the van tonight and get a fresh start tomorrow."

Xander looked back up the path that led to the van.

When he turned back to me, his face was calmer. "It'll be fine. I'll be okay."

I nodded. "We both will."

When I dropped my hands, he looked down at them as if he wanted them back. They probably felt like a weighted blanket against his fears.

"I think we need to take a ninety-degree turn up here." I flipped my light back on and nearly plowed into a man standing straight in our path.

He screamed. I screamed. Xander and another person screamed.

When our screams had left our throats and were mere echoes on the cliff faces around us, I said, "Who are you, and what are you doing here?"

A woman peeked out from behind the man and said, "We're trying to get back to our car before dark. We didn't bring any headlamps or flashlights, and we got lost."

I sucked in a breath and tried to calm my heartbeat. "You'll want to head back up this trail. Stay to the left. There's a cliff edge to the right." I took my pack off and dug inside it until I found my extra flashlight. "Take this. It'll help you get out."

The man took the flashlight.

"Thank you so much," the woman said. "Is your car parked up in the lot? We can leave it there for you."

"Yep," I said. "It's the VW Microbus. Her name's Mona." I didn't remember seeing another car in the lot, but I hadn't been looking either.

The woman smiled. "See, I told you we should name our cars. It makes them sound so much friendlier."

The man didn't smile. In fact, he looked downright angry.

"Are the two of you heading back to the parking lot, too?" the man asked.

"No, we—"

"Not yet," Xander interrupted, stepping in front of me. "We forgot something on the trail, but we'll be heading back shortly."

"We didn't see anything on the trail," the woman said. "What are you looking for?"

"We went a bit off the trail and left a camera," Xander said. "It shouldn't take but a few more minutes. We'll probably even catch up to you on the way out."

The man grabbed the woman's hand and pulled her past us.

"Thanks again for the flashlight," she said.

"Why did you lie to them?" I asked when they were out of earshot.

"Why would you want to tell them the truth? They're perfect strangers out in the wilderness at night."

I shook my head and retook the lead. The red trail was fading in my mind, but still there. "We have to hurry. The trail is lessening."

"Does that mean something happened to her?" Xander asked. "Shouldn't it be getting more pronounced as we get closer?"

"How should I know?" I asked. "I've never tracked anyone like this. When I tracked Renée, there was no trail to her."

"That's probably because she's the Grand Witch. She likely had tracking spells blocked."

I turned and gave him a suspicious glance. "Right, like I could override the Grand Witch's block."

Xander slipped and let out a yelp.

"Are you okay?"

"I'm fine," he said. "Just thought I was going to go over the edge of the cliff."

"The cliff is behind us," I said, shining my light toward the trees. "We must be above a cave or something."

The red streak went off the path and down into the trees.

"Where are you going?" Xander asked as I veered off the path.

"Come on. It's okay."

We walked in silence for a while. Down and up and down again until we were at the mouth of a cave.

"Looks like this is where we need to go," I said. "Maybe she's hiding in here."

"We're going inside the cave?"

"If you don't want to, you can stay out here."

He looked around. "Maybe I'll just guard the entrance. If you yell, I'll come running."

"Deal," I said. It was slightly adorable that he was scared. He rarely showed any weakness.

The trail into the cave started with a steep slope of mud. I slid down as if I was on a snowboard and hoped my foot wouldn't catch a stray rock. Thankfully, I made it to the bottom without falling.

I shined my headlamp around to see the cave was massive. The air was easily ten degrees cooler, and I could see my breath coming out in little white puffs.

Bats flew in and out, and stalactites hung from the ceiling. The floor was more like a little stream with rocks interspersed. I tried to stay on the rocks, but every once in a while, my foot made the plunge into the river, sending cold water through my shoe and into my socks. Thank goodness I brought a few extra pairs.

The red streak was little more than a pink cloud in my mind's eye now, but either way, it had led me to this cave. It might take some time exploring each nook and cranny, but I knew Melly May was inside.

Or maybe it wouldn't take long at all.

The sound of a woman's scream broke the silence. It echoed all around me, but from where it had come, I had no clue.

"Melly May?"

"Ellie?" Xander yelled.

"I'm okay," I said. "Did you hear the scream too?"

"Yeah," his voice echoed. "Did it come from in there or—"

He didn't finish his sentence other than with a couple of curse words and a splash.

Whether or not he wanted to be, Xander was now in the cave.

8

I hurried to the mouth of the cave to find Xander sitting in the creek, soaking wet and shaking.

"Are you okay?" I asked, holding a hand out for him.

He seemed frozen to the spot. His eyes squinted shut.

I crouched down and put a hand on his shoulder. Again, anxiety crept up through my palm, but this time it was overwhelming. He was having an anxiety attack.

I sucked in a breath and focused on calm—Penelope's soft nose, Mona's warm steering wheel, the everlasting lilac wreath on my bedroom door. In and out, in and out, I breathed until I could feel the anxiety dissipating.

"I'm here," I said. "You're safe. I'm safe. Everything is okay."

Eventually, our breathing matched up, and Xander opened his eyes. "I'm slightly claustrophobic."

That explained why he didn't want to be inside the cave.

"Let's get you out of here," I said.

"But someone screamed. We need to help them."

"I don't know where the screaming came from. Right now, the only person I need to help is you."

"I'm okay," Xander finally said. "I'm cold and wet, but I'm okay."

He and I stood, and he ventured a glance up to the ceiling. "It's taller than I expected." He took a couple of deep breaths. "As long as it stays like this, I think I'll be okay."

I wasn't sure how far back the cave went, but I had to take him at his word. If he had another attack, I'd be there to help him.

We ventured farther into the cave, careful to stay on the rocks. With each step, it seemed to get colder.

"Are you sure the scream came from back here?" Xander asked, his teeth chattering between words.

"No," I said. "But I'm sure Melly May is back here."

"If she's the one who screamed, there was probably a reason," Xander said. "Be on your guard."

Oh, I was definitely on my guard.

As the cave narrowed, I could hear Xander's breaths coming shorter and quicker.

"I think she's this way," I said, pointing to a narrow opening in the cave wall that led down a tight crevice. "Why don't you stay out here."

"But what if something is in there?"

"Then make sure to get it on the way out." I dropped my pack on the ground at his feet.

He didn't look convinced, but his phobia was keeping him from objecting to my plan.

As I crawled into the fissure, my scalp tingled. She was here. I knew it.

My lamp shined brightly off the walls until the beam came upon a sight I wished I'd never seen.

I sucked in a breath and clapped a dirty hand over my mouth.

"Are you okay?" Xander yelled behind me. "Was it her? Did she scream?"

The woman in front of me most definitely did not scream. Though she still had patches of hair, clothes, and even some skin on her bones, it was apparent she had been dead for quite some time.

"Ellie?" Xander yelled again, this time with more panic in his voice.

"I'm okay," I said. "I don't know if it's Melly May, but there's a body back here."

Then the light from my headlamp reflected off something. I didn't want to touch anything, but her necklace looked familiar.

A knot twisted in my stomach. I knew who she was, and she wasn't Melly May.

9

I crawled back out of the crevice with tears welling up in my eyes.

"What did you find?" Xander asked. "What's wrong?"

"I think it's—" I couldn't say the last word. If I said it, it would make it true.

I dug into my backpack and pulled out the one thing I took with me everywhere—a photocopy of the picture of my mother and me.

And there, around her neck, was the same necklace as the woman in the crevice wore.

"Who, El?" Xander asked. "Who is she?"

"Emily." I handed him the photo. "They have the same necklace."

Xander looked at the photo. "No, that can't be right. You saw your mother in a tunnel."

"Or a cave," I said, motioning around us. "And I bet when the sun is up, there's a pinprick of light coming from that direction."

"What about the sound of the train?" Xander asked.

We listened for a moment, but it was silent.

"Maybe when the wind comes through." I shrugged and wiped a tear from my face. I never thought I'd find my mother like this. I'd never be able to ask her any questions. Never be able to figure out why she left me all those years ago.

"I think we should get out of here," Xander said. "We'll bring the police back tomorrow."

"But what about Melly May," I said, sniffling.

"Do you still think she's here?" He glanced around. "Or do you think maybe your magic mistook all those times you asked about your mom and led you here?"

"I don't know," I said. "I just don't know."

I closed my eyes and focused, but the tears in my eyes prevented me from seeing anything with my magic. I was tired and sad, and my magic no longer wanted to work.

"What about the scream?" Xander asked. "Maybe that was Melly May."

"Well, we're pretty much at a dead-end here," I said. The rest of the cave was just a wall and another crevice that looked far too small for a person to fit inside. "Let's go back and call the police."

Xander offered me his hand, but I didn't want to take it. I needed to be in my feelings alone right now.

Thankfully, he seemed to understand as he led the way back out of the cave. When we reached the steep muddy incline, Xander tried to make it up but couldn't. The mud was too slick.

"That's fantastic," Xander muttered.

I took out my phone, hoping I'd have service so we could call someone, but there was none.

"Here," I said, shoving my phone back in my jeans pocket. "I'll try."

I took a running start, but before I even made it to the muddy slope, my foot caught between a couple of rocks, and my ankle twisted. My body crumpled to the ground as I let out a yelp in pain.

Xander was instantly at my side.

I yanked on my leg, but I couldn't get my foot out without pain shooting through my ankle. "It's stuck."

Xander held his hands over the rocks, and they moved.

My foot slipped out, but there was no way I was walking on it, let alone climbing a muddy incline.

A crack of lightning and the instantaneous thunder shook the walls around us. Then came the rain.

Or rather, downpour.

And there was the sound—the train.

"We have to get to higher ground," Xander said, lifting me as if I was as light as a feather.

"There's a ledge back there," I said, trying not to think about the fact that my mother was dead. "It's probably big enough to set up a tent or at least some sleeping bags for the night."

"You want to sleep down here?" Xander stopped in his tracks.

"I don't know what else to do," I said. "I won't be able to make it up that incline and—with the rain coming in like that—neither will you. We're better off staying dry and waiting until morning."

"Staying dry?" Xander scoffed.

"I brought extra clothes," I said. "Several pairs. My clothes might be too small for you, but they stretch."

"I have my own clothes," Xander said. "But where will we change?"

This caught me off guard. Xander was always such a flirt. It was probably because he was dating Laura now.

"I can help set up the tent," I said. "Even though we won't need it in here."

"Other than to protect us from the bats."

"The bats won't hurt us."

"They might nibble on our toes."

This made me laugh for a split second. Then I remembered my mother was in the same tunnel as us. At least, her body was.

As we set up the tent, I asked, "Do you believe in ghosts?"

"Sure," Xander said. "Ghosts are as real as you and me."

"Really? Have you seen one before?"

Xander secured one pole into the loop and then stood to look at me. "You can't tell me you believe in magic, but you don't believe in ghosts."

"What else should I believe in?" I asked. "Aliens? Sasquatch? The Easter Bunny?"

"Don't be ridiculous," Xander said. "Those are all made up to scare kids into being good."

"What kind of childhood did you have?" I asked.

"A perfect one if you ask my father," he said. "But seriously, ghosts are real."

"Do you think the ghost of my mother lives in this cave?"

"I've only ever met one ghost before," Xander said. "And I met her far from where she died, so I wouldn't bet on Emily being here."

"Oh," I said. That meant that if my mother had died a while ago, she could have been a ghost anywhere. Like with me.

Even in the afterlife, she chose not to be with me.

I stretched my neck, loosening the thoughts from my head.

I wouldn't think that way. I couldn't let myself go down the pity party route. I promised myself a long time ago that even if I never met my mother, I wouldn't let her define my life.

My life was mine to live. I would make the most of it.

10

Xander finished the tent while I pulled out some of the hot soup I'd brought in my thermos. It wasn't much, but it would give us a tiny bit of energy.

I'd changed in the tent first, careful not to hurt my ankle. Then Xander changed, and now we were both in the tiny tent together, eating soup in the dark.

"Are you sure you don't want me to turn on my head-lamp?" I asked.

"When it's dark, I can pretend we're not in a tent inside of a cave that might start flooding at any moment."

Every part of me wished he wasn't dating Laura. That he'd pull me into his lap and keep me warm through the night. But I had to respect their relationship, even if I didn't like it.

"How's your ankle?" Xander asked, his voice almost a whisper.

"It's feeling better," I said. He'd soaked my dirty shirt in the cold water, so I had the closest thing to an ice compress. "I think I just twisted it. I'll be better tomorrow."

"Do you really think the woman back there is your mother? Maybe someone has a necklace like hers."

"I got this feeling that she was who I was looking for."

"Maybe she was Melly May."

I thought about it for a minute. "I guess she could have been. But what about the necklace?"

"She could have had the same one," Xander said. "It's possible."

"It was creepy," I said. "Her hair was still there and parts of her skin. It was like she crawled up in here and died."

"Maybe she did," Xander said.

"Let's talk about something else."

"Sounds good to me." Xander shifted, and I held my breath, hoping his hand might brush against mine. But it didn't.

"How are you and Laura?" I asked.

"We're—uh—good," he said. "Tell me more about you and Bernardo."

"I figured you knew most of it since you're the one who practically set us up."

He mumbled something under his breath.

"What?" I asked.

"Nothing," he said. "Bernardo is a bit of a player, so be careful."

"You know, when I first met you, I thought you were a bit of a player too."

"Maybe it runs in the family."

"I hope, for Jake's sake, it doesn't," I said.

"Georgia is an exception to the rule," Xander said. "When she first showed up in town, I figured she was spying on me for my parents—we don't talk anymore. But if they wanted to spy on me, they probably wouldn't have asked Georgia to do it."

"Why not?"

"Because Georgia's always been on my side," he said. "And they'd use someone much sneakier."

"It sounds like your parents care about you."

"That's pretty much their job description." He clapped a hand over his mouth. "I'm so sorry, El. I didn't—"

"It's okay," I said. "I don't know the whole situation with my mom. Who even knows who my dad is? And none of my foster parents got to know me very well."

"It always impresses me how you see things."

"How is that?"

"You give everyone the benefit of the doubt. You never see the bad in people—even people who have done terrible things. And you take life as if it was one big adventure."

"That's because my life has been one big adventure."

"Sometimes I wish I hadn't been so sheltered—so brought up in the magical world," Xander said. "The non-magical world is wonderful too."

"Did you live in an all-magical city or something?"

"Something like that," he said. "It's hard to explain. Some cities have more magical folk than others, but I grew up in a place where there were only the magical. Like the magical capital of the United States."

"Where is that on the map?" I laughed.

"It's in the Rocky Mountains—up in Rocky Mountain

National Park. Well, the entry to it is. The actual city isn't really in the mountains."

"That's crazy," I said. "I hiked so many times in Rocky Mountain National Park."

"You probably felt comfortable there."

Now that he mentioned it, I did. "Do you think that's why my mother left me at a fire station in Colorado?"

Xander didn't reply.

"Xander?"

"I don't think I want to guess about why your mother did anything."

"It's probably better that way." I yawned. I didn't want to go to sleep while Xander was practically spilling his guts about his personal life, but my eyelids weren't going to stay open much longer. "How will we sleep in here?"

"I figured we'd sleep with our feet at each other's heads."

"I hope Laura doesn't get angry at you for this."

"She won't," Xander said.

11

I was falling. Soaking wet. Or maybe I was flying in the rain.

The rain was backward. It came from the ground and went to the sky.

I closed my eyes. Something was wrong. I could feel it.

Where was the cave? Where was Xander?

Where was my mom?

Emily.

Emily Vanderwick.

A light flashed in front of my face.

"You're pregnant," a voice echoed in my head.

Elation pulsed through my body.

Then fear.

"You have to," another voice whispered.

No.

I couldn't.

The air turned bright orange.

Flames.

It was hot. Really hot.

And cold.

I was shivering.

Emily.

Where was Emily?

The sound of a train rumbling through a tunnel blasted in my ears.

I screamed.

Get out of the tunnel before the train hits you!

I tried to say the words, but they wouldn't come out of my mouth.

The ground was hard beneath me, but something held me tight.

Emily?

Mom?

"Ellie," a voice echoed behind me.

I tried to turn but couldn't.

My ankle seared in pain as I tried to get up.

"Don't get up," Xander's voice came closer. "You're having a bad dream."

My heart raced as I opened my eyes.

It was dark.

There was no fire.

Xander was holding me as I sobbed and shook.

"It's okay," Xander said. "I'm here."

He pressed a kiss to the top of my head, and the shaking stopped.

"I don't think the woman in the cave is Emily," I said. "I think she's still alive."

"That's great," Xander said, smoothing down my hair.

"I'm sorry if I woke you."

"I think you woke up the entire state park with that

scream." He laughed. "But from what I can tell, the rain has stopped, and the sun will probably be up in less than an hour."

I rolled over to face him, his arms still wrapped around me. He was so warm. So comforting. I didn't want him to let me go.

But he was going to. He had to. He had a girlfriend. And we were just fr—

His lips on mine stopped my thoughts short. Xander's kiss was gentle and slow, but it sparked like a field of fireflies—here, there, and everywhere.

"Is someone down here?" a man's voice came from the mouth of the cave.

Xander's lips detached from mine, and I took a breath to steady myself.

"We are," Xander said, unzipping the tent.

"Have you seen my wife?" the man asked. "We got lost last night. I heard her scream, but I can't find her."

"Is it the guy from the couple we saw?" I whispered.

Xander peeked out of the tent. "It looks like it."

"Maybe he can help us out of here, and we can help him find his wife."

Xander stopped me when I started to get up. "What if he's dangerous?"

"Wouldn't he have done something to us in the dark rather than waiting until the next morning?"

"Good point," he said. "How does your ankle feel?"

I looked down. It was pretty swollen. "I can probably walk on it."

"Hello?" the man called again.

"We haven't seen your wife," Xander said, standing

and then helping me come to a stand outside of the tent. "We've been stuck in this cave all night."

My ankle was tender, but it wasn't anything I couldn't handle.

"Give us a minute to pack up, and maybe you can help us out of here," Xander said.

"Sure thing," the man said.

Xander and I packed up the tent and the rest of the things we'd unpacked the night before.

"Ready?" I asked, trying not to be awkward about our kiss.

"Just one more thing," Xander said. He wrapped an arm around my waist and pulled me toward him, kissing me more passionately this time.

Tingles ran from my lips to every other part of my body. My hair most certainly was changing, and my heart felt like it might explode. I couldn't believe he was kissing me. For real. Without an ulterior motive, like changing my hair back to normal.

When he pulled back, the smile on his lips probably matched my own. "That's nice," he said. "We should do it more often."

"What about Laura?" I asked, unable to stop the words from coming out of my mouth.

Xander turned back to me. "I should have told you last night, but my pride got in the way. Laura dumped me. Via text. That's why I was so grumpy when you called."

Part of me was thrilled he hadn't just cheated on his girlfriend by kissing me, but the other part felt like the rebound. I'd had enough rebounds in my life to know what they looked like. And as much as I wanted to kiss

Xander over and over again, I couldn't let it happen like this.

"What's wrong?" Xander asked.

"Nothing," I said.

"Your hair gave you away." His gaze flickered to my head and back to my eyes.

"I just don't want to be your rebound," I said. "You seemed pretty broken up about Laura."

"That's understandable," Xander said. "But what if I told you I only ever really wanted to be with yo—"

"Are you guys still packing up down there?" the man interrupted. "I think it's about to rain again."

"Let's talk about this later," Xander said. "When we're not trapped under tons and tons of rock and dirt."

Was he about to say that he only ever wanted to be with me? But then why had he friend-zoned me so many times? It made absolutely no sense.

"El, you coming?" Xander turned around and smiled at me, turning my insides into mush.

I stood and almost fell on my bad ankle, but I took a deep breath and pushed on.

"How will we get up the muddy slope?" I asked as Xander, and I looked up at the obstacle that had kept us down there in the first place.

"Come over to this side," the man at the top of the slope said. "There's a hidden stairway of sorts. You'll have to walk through the creek to get there."

Xander helped me through the cold water, his touch electrifying as usual. Why did it matter if I was a rebound? Surely lots of people stayed together after being the rebounds. Especially if he had liked me first.

Around the side of a rock was a rock staircase, exactly like the man had said.

"Thanks for the help," Xander said when we got to the top. "I'm Xander, and this is Ellie."

"Orson." The man was bigger than I remembered from the night before.

"It's nice to meet yo—" I started, but he cut me off.

"Are you going to help me find my wife or not?"

"Where's the last place you saw her?" Xander asked Orson.

The sun was peeking up over the cliffs, creating a sort of mist that hung in the air just above the ground. It was serene. Until the man started speaking again.

"She was with me when we saw you." Orson's voice boomed through the caves with each syllable. "We were heading toward the car when she saw a mushroom. She plucked it from the ground and ate it. Told me it was a delicacy. I don't eat mushrooms, but she made me try it." He took a breath. "It was disgusting and made me feel funny. But we kept going to the car. We were almost there when I heard her scream and realized she wasn't behind me."

"How do you know it was her scream?" I asked. "Could it have been another woman?"

"I know my wife's voice." He took a step toward me,

and Xander instinctively put himself between the man and me.

"What happened when you heard her scream?" Xander asked.

"I ran back into the park," Orson said. "I couldn't find her. I yelled and yelled, but she didn't say anything else."

He yelled, and we hadn't heard him? I looked him over more closely. Caked-on mud covered from the bottom of his shoes to the middle of his shins. His jacket was tied around his waist, and his bare arms looked like they had been scraped up by the rocks . . . or possibly by his wife.

I shook my head. Why in the world would I think such a thing? If he'd hurt his wife, wouldn't he have just left? I mean, the woman in the cave hadn't been discovered for this long. Who knew how long it would take us to find his wife?

Not that she was necessarily dead.

"You okay?" Xander asked, a worried look on his face.

"Just not feeling myself," I said. "It's okay."

I'd probably just seen too much murder in the past year. When I'd moved to Cliff Haven, I didn't realize how much my life would change. Or how many dead bodies I'd come across. My mind was bound to jump to conclusions every now and again.

"What part of the park have you already searched?" I asked.

Orson looked around. "It all looks the same to me. I passed out after looking for a while. The mushrooms were probably poisonous. Maybe Jerri passed out and fell off a cliff."

"If she passed out, how would she have screamed?" I asked.

Orson narrowed his eyes at me. "Are you insinuating something?" His voice was deep and quiet. Anger and fear overwhelmed me. Thankfully, I had on a hat. I wasn't sure what might trip this guy's trigger.

"She's not insinuating anything," Xander said. "She's worked with the police on several cases recently, so her natural inclination is to go to questioning."

"You're a cop?" Orson boomed.

"Not a cop," I said. "A recreational therapist who occasionally helps the police. And I'd like to help you find your wife if that's okay with you."

My words held a bit more snark than usual, but I wouldn't let this guy stomp all over me.

"Let's head toward the parking lot and see what we can find," Xander said.

I held Xander back so Orson could take the lead. If he had something to do with his wife's disappearance, he would probably steer us away from her body. Or maybe he'd steer us right toward it and act surprised when we found her.

I stopped in my tracks. Hadn't Xander just told me the night before how much he appreciated my ability to see the good in people? And here I was, making assumptions about a man I didn't know. Why? Because he intimidated me?

That was ridiculous. I'd been around men more intimidating than him. Plus, his wife might be perfectly fine. We didn't know. Maybe she saw a snake, screamed, and hid.

I resumed my slow pace, letting the two men lead the

way several yards ahead of me. My ankle was either getting better or was simply numb to the pain. If it was the latter, I'd pay for it later. Maybe the morning sessions wouldn't be walks for a while after all.

"I think the parking lot is up this hill and to the right," Orson said.

I pulled out my phone, which was on low battery and had zero service. If only I could see where we were on a map.

"Did either of you bring a GPS unit?" I asked.

Orson looked at me like I'd grown another head. "We were going on a short early morning hike. That's what Jerri said. A short hike. To stretch our legs. Why would we need a GPS unit for a short hike?" Whether I saw a tear in his eye or I'd made it up in my mind so I could find some sort of compassion for the man who was yelling was beyond me, but either way, I reminded myself—hurting people hurt people.

He was probably a nice man in different situations.

"That makes total sense," I said calmly. "Xander, you didn't bring one, did you?"

Xander shook his head. "I didn't realize how convoluted the trail system would be."

Orson started to walk again. "If only we could find that pregnant volunteer. She seemed to know her way around."

Xander held back, and when Orson was out of hearing range, Xander asked, "Do you think you could use your tracking magic to find the car? Or his wife?"

"My tracking magic can only detect other magic. Did you sense his wife was magical?"

"No," Xander said. "But if it can detect other magic,

can it detect its own magic?"

"I'm not sure I understand what you're asking."

"Like, can you focus on your own magic trail—or mine —and see where we've been?"

It was a long shot, but it could be possible. Heck, anything could be possible.

I closed my eyes and steadied my breathing. Without my sight, the smell of the damp leaves and the mud flooded my senses.

My trail was pink and gold. Interesting. I hadn't considered different magical trails would have different colors. And Xander's was a deep blue, almost black, with flecks of silver in it.

I followed the trail back to the cave, where a large cloud of our trail hung. The trail that emerged was weaker. It had cooled, but I could see it.

It led to the left of where we stood.

"We need to take a left at the next fork in the trail," I said.

"Good job." The pride in Xander's smile warmed every part of me, even the tips of my toes that were still frozen in my wet shoes. Growing up without a steady home life meant I didn't have many people say they were proud of me. Occasionally, I'd have a teacher or boss who was, but eventually, I'd leave the class or the job and those moments behind.

"Orson," Xander called out, not taking his gaze off me. "We need to take a left up here at the fork in the trail."

"How did you know there was a fork in the trail?" Orson bellowed back.

"I didn't," Xander said. "Ellie did."

13

Once we took a left at the fork, the parking lot was only about a half-mile ahead of us.

Orson didn't look pleased when we got there. "Where's my car?"

Sure enough, the only vehicle in the parking lot was Mona, who looked shiny and almost refreshed from the rainstorm.

"That no good—" Orson started calling his wife every name in the book.

When he seemed to be finished, Xander laid a hand on Orson's shoulder. "Let's think about this for a moment."

"Think about what?" Orson pushed his hand away. "My wife giving me a poisonous mushroom, pretending she was in trouble, then taking off in my car?" Orson was getting huffy again, but Xander kept his voice neutral.

"Let's think about another possibility," Xander said. "Perhaps, your wife *is* in trouble, and someone stole your car."

"My car was nothing special," Orson said. "But I guess it's better than that pile of garbage over there."

Anger flared through me so swiftly, I didn't know what I was doing until Xander grabbed my arm.

Orson's glare turned to a smile. Then he was doubled over laughing.

Fire was in my veins. How dare he insult Mona?

"You thought you were going to hit me?" Orson gasped for air between his words and his laughter.

Xander dropped my hand and shook his as if my touch had burned him. "El, you need to control your magic right now."

"Mona is a good van," I whispered.

"Stupid women. Naming their cars." Orson gasped for air through his laughter and words.

If he wasn't careful, he'd be gasping for air through my fingertips.

"Ellie Vanderwick." Xander stepped between Orson and me, this time protecting him. "Take a breath. This man is not worth a life spent in prison."

Orson stopped laughing and peeked over Xander's shoulder. "You don't really think she could hurt me, do you?"

"Orson, go away," Xander said.

"But she's just a tiny little—"

Xander turned and yelled right in Orson's face. "GO!"

Orson might not have been scared of me, but he was certainly scared of Xander.

He nearly tripped on his own shoes as he backed up to get away from us.

"You're both nuts," Orson yelled, his voice now filled with fear. "Stay away from me."

Xander didn't respond. He turned back to me and took my hands in his. "It's okay. Remember last night when you told me to breathe? I need you to do that for me now."

I turned my focus from Orson to Xander.

He and I breathed together until my heart rate had gone back to normal. That's when the regret hit. "What just happened?"

"You were defending something—someone—you love. Mona is like family to you, and that imbecile was bad-mouthing her." He pulled me into a hug. "It's only normal that your magic would want to end him."

"But my magic can't do that, right?" I asked. "Magic can't kill people."

"Your magic can't because of who you are," Xander said. "But there have been a handful of times in our history when magic was used to kill someone else."

This didn't make me feel much better. If it had happened before, that meant it could happen again. And who was he to say I didn't have it in me? When Orson had said those things, every part of me wanted to hurt him.

Warm tears trickled down my face. Who was I becoming? Was my magic making me into a monster?

"Let's get to Mona and warm up," Xander said. "Maybe if we drive out of the trees, we'll get service."

"What about Orson?" I asked. "We can't just leave him out here."

"We'll pick him up on the way. I would guess he's a good mile down the road by now."

I slid into the driver's seat but realized almost instantly I wouldn't be able to drive. "My ankle is too tender to push the pedals," I said, hopping back out. "I think you'll have to drive."

Xander seemed surprised by this but took the keys and the driver's seat after helping me into the passenger side.

"Let's hope she starts for me," Xander said with a nervous laugh.

No one else had ever driven her. Not since I'd purchased her from a green-eyed man when I was sixteen. "Do you have family in the used car business?" I asked as Xander put the keys in the ignition.

"I'm not sure," Xander said, turning the key in the ignition.

Mona didn't even try to start. It was as if she had a dead battery.

"That's weird," Xander said, his eyes focused on the gauges in front of him. "The lights came on when we got in, didn't they?"

I opened my door, and the dome light came on.

"I guess that means the battery isn't dead." Xander tried again, but still, Mona was silent. "Is there a trick to this?"

I grabbed the metal steering wheel with the lilac etchings. It warmed to my touch. "Come on, Mona. I can't drive, so Xander will take us back to Cliff Haven."

Xander turned the key again. This time she made some rumbling noises, but the engine still didn't start.

"Maybe I should get out and take a look," I said, wincing with every movement of my ankle.

"Ellie, wait." Xander's voice was quiet, distant.

I turned to find him staring down at the dash. "What is it?"

"I lied to you."

My mind raced with possibilities. He was still dating Laura. He wasn't a good warlock. He killed people for a living.

"My family *is* in the used car business, along with just about every business known to man."

A bubble of laughter burst from my mouth. "That's it? That's the lie?"

"I think that's why Mona won't start for me," he said.

"If that's the case, she should start now that you told me the truth, right?"

"Is there a reason you asked me that question?" Xander asked, still not looking at me.

I thought back to why I asked. The green eyes. "The man who sold her to me—"

"Is my father."

"Gerald is your father?" My insides twisted. "How long have you known?"

"Since before I met you," Xander said. "But I can't say anything else. My family's business is rather secretive."

"I knew that place was magical," I said. "He didn't even let me pay. I had the money, but the office was closed, and when I went back the next day, I couldn't even find the lot."

"You were meant to have Mona," Xander said. "My father just made it so."

"Well, I'd like to thank him for that and to pay him what I owe."

"Maybe someday you will be able to, but right now we need to—"

"Right now, we need to do nothing," I interrupted. "Right now, I need you to be honest with me. Is that the only time you've lied? I thought you said you'd never lie to me."

"That's the only time," Xander said. "But I understand why you wouldn't trust me. That's why I make it a point not to lie. And that's why I got out of the family business. It's centered around secrecy, and secrets are practically lies."

"But you have plenty of secrets."

"Everyone deserves their privacy."

"That is true," I said.

"I'm really sorry, El."

"When you said you knew before you met me, how did you know? Like, were you there when it happened? Or did your dad tell you?"

He shook his head. "I can't say. I don't want to lie to you again, but it's not my place to tell you all these things."

"Then take me to your father," I said. "I want to know what the heck is going on."

"I don't know where he is right now. And we have a dead body to report."

He was right, but I didn't want to accept it. "Fine, but I want to meet him just as soon as you know where he is."

"I don't know that I can make that promise."

I crossed my arms over my chest.

"I'll do what I can," Xander said.

That was as good as I was going to get. I could feel it.

"Mona, please start for him."

He turned the key, and she started right up.

"Thank you."

Xander smiled. "She's quite the van."

"Yes, she is."

Xander drove out of the parking lot and back onto the gravel road.

"Did your dad get you a special car when you turned sixteen?"

"This is exactly why I didn't want to talk about my personal life." Xander sighed. "Can we skip the questions, please?"

I huffed. He didn't have to act like I was an annoying little kid.

I stared out the side window and watched as the farms and fields passed by. Then Xander started accelerating.

"Why are you going so fast?" I asked.

But when I looked over at Xander, he seemed as startled as I was. "I'm not. Mona is." He had a death grip on the steering wheel and his foot on the brake. The brake that was not depressing at all regardless of how hard he stomped on it.

"Mona, stop. He said he was sorry," I said. "You'll kill us both."

But she wasn't stopping.

"Look." Xander took one hand off the wheel and pointed at something ahead of us.

"Is that Orson?"

"He's walking on the side of the road." Xander put his hand back on the wheel. "She's going to run him over."

"Mona, no," I said. "Do not run that man over. I know he said mean things about you, but if you run him over, Xander will be at fault."

I was shocked this was happening. Mona always seemed to have a mind of her own, but she'd never taken control like this.

"And I know you're probably still mad at me for lying," Xander said. "But I promise I won't lie to Ellie again. Please, don't put me in jail for one simple little lie."

But Mona wasn't stopping. She wasn't even slowing. She was accelerating.

"Your tires will lose traction on this gravel," I said. "We'll flip."

I grabbed the steering wheel. It was as hot as my blood had been when Orson had been talking trash about Mona. "Come on. You don't want to do this."

The wheel turned, aiming for Orson head-on.

He must have heard the engine coming up behind him because he held out an arm with his thumb in the air.

Why was he hitchhiking when we were the only ones that were in the park—the only ones who could have been coming from our direction?

Within seconds, we would hit him.

"Mona." I gripped the wheel tighter and tried to turn it away from Orson. "Stop!"

Orson glanced behind him, his eyes widening at the sight of my sweet—and salty—van barreling toward him.

He threw his arms in the air to cover his face at the same time the wheel jerked out of my hands.

We skidded to a stop, and the side door flew open just before we came into contact with Orson.

"I think she wants you to get in," Xander said, his voice shaky.

Orson probably thought Xander was talking about me, but Xander and I both knew he was talking about Mona.

"Why would I get in with you?" Orson spat. "You nearly ran me over."

"Nearly," Xander said with a shrug, trying to play it all off. "We didn't, though."

"I'm calling the police just as soon as I get service." Orson pulled out his phone and waved it at us. "You two are going to jail."

"How about we save you the minutes," I said. "We're headed to the police station right now."

"This is a trick—a trap," Orson said. "I'm fine. I'll walk."

The moment he turned from the door, the sky opened up, and hail the size of golf balls came pouring down.

With every hit, Orson cowered, his arms above his head, trying to deflect the projectiles. Mona would definitely have hail damage from this storm.

I reached over to the steering wheel. "I'll fix whatever damage you get. Thank you for not running him over."

"Are you coming or not?" Xander yelled over the sound.

Orson jumped in the back. "I'll come, but I'm warning you, I have pepper spray, and I'm not afraid to use it."

The door closed without Orson so much as touching it. I held back a laugh when I saw the surprise on his face.

"Let's go to the police station," I said.

Xander pushed on the gas, and Mona accelerated at a normal speed. Xander exhaled loudly, then said, "Thanks, Mona."

Deb was walking out the police station doors as we were walking in. The hail had stopped just as quickly as it had started, and the sun was out in full force.

"I want to report these two for almost running me over," Orson said when he saw her badge.

Deb raised her eyebrows at Xander and me. "Is that so?"

"He's right," Xander said. "The van was out of control, and we almost hit him."

"Thankfully, Mona stopped just in time," I said.

"So, you didn't mean to almost hit this man?" Deb asked.

"No," Xander said. "We absolutely didn't want to hit him."

"They were headed right toward me," Orson said. "I could hear their engine picking up speed."

"But they didn't hit you?" Deb asked.

"They almost did." Orson's voice was that of defeat.

"We're sorry we scared you," I said.

"At least we gave you a ride back to town," Xander said.

"Let me get this straight," Deb said. "You thought they were going to hit you with their van, but when they stopped, you got in and let them give you a ride?"

"It was hailing," Orson said. "I could feel the bruises forming. I had no choice."

Deb looked up at the clear blue sky. "If I was afraid for my life, I'd take hail over death."

Orson didn't reply. His face was bright red.

"Can I help you with anything else?" Deb asked, her face brightening into a smile.

"We need to talk to you," I said. "In private."

"No way." Orson pushed me to the side and got right between Xander and Deb. "I get to go first. My wife stole my car and tried to poison me."

Deb's face went from cheery to intimidating in a millisecond. "Please, keep your hands to yourself, sir."

Orson's fists tightened at his sides like he wanted to punch her.

"I am happy to talk to each of you when I return to the station." Deb walked past Orson, Xander, and me and opened the door to her police car.

"But my wife—" Orson started.

"We'll find your wife, sir," Deb said. "I'll be back shortly." She shut her car door, turned on her lights and sirens, and squealed out of the parking lot.

"Stupid podunk police department," Orson said. "I'm going to go inside and speak to the chief himself."

"He's on vacation," I said. "But you can call him on my cell if you want."

I pulled my phone out of the pocket of my jeans and realized it was dead.

"Oh sorry, maybe Xander has his number."

Xander shook his head. "My phone's dead too."

Orson huffed and barged into the station, leaving Xander and me outside alone.

"Did you do that thing with the weather?" I asked.

Xander laughed. "Don't you think if I could control the weather, I would have done so last night?"

"Good point."

"Maybe Mona did it," Xander said.

"Did you know she could do that?" I asked. "Since your father . . ."

Xander shook his head. "I've never known a car—even a magical one—to take control like that. The two of you must have a special connection."

I glanced over at Mona. She didn't look even slightly damaged by the hail. Maybe she had controlled the weather. Or perhaps it was a lucky coincidence.

Deb pulled back into the parking lot, this time with her lights and siren off. "Come on, get out," she said to someone in the passenger seat.

The door opened, and Misty stepped out. She wasn't in uniform and looked like she'd had about five too many drinks.

"Are you mad at me?" Misty asked, her words slurred.

"We'll talk about it inside," Deb said. "You need a cup of coffee to sober up, and I need to talk to some people."

"Hi, Ellie," Misty said. She had dried blood on her forehead.

"Hey, Misty," I said with a smile. "Are you okay?"

"Just a flesh wound." Misty laughed.

Deb shook her head. "Come on in. I'll be with you in a couple of minutes." She and Misty walked through a locked door.

Orson was standing by the reception desk. "Does anyone actually work here?"

"Deb said she'd be right back," I said.

Orson turned back to me slowly. "Deb? You have the police chief's phone number in your phone, and you know the officers by their first names?"

"It's a small town." I shrugged. "Practically everyone knows everyone else."

"I told you before, Ellie helps the police," Xander said.

"This is ridiculous," Orson said. "There's no way I'll get an unbiased ear here. You have these people in your back pocket. I'll take my business to the next town over."

"Unfortunately," Deb said, emerging from the hallway she'd just walked down. "You were likely in my jurisdiction when the crime occurred. Therefore, the town over will simply send you back here."

"Then I'll call the FBI," Orson said. "They have jurisdiction everywhere. They'll come in here and rip my case right out from under you."

Deb shrugged, her palms up. "You can call the FBI."

"That's what I'll do then." Orson hesitated a split second before turning and walking out the doors.

Deb turned her attention to Xander and me. "Please

tell me you haven't found another dead body in your cornfield."

"Not in my cornfield," I said.

"This day just keeps getting better and better." She sighed. "Come on back."

"Let me make sure I understand you," Deb said after we'd told her the entire story. "You somehow—don't tell me the details—but you somehow tracked Melly May and found a slightly decomposed body inside a cave?"

Xander and I nodded.

"And you thought it was your mother because the body was wearing a necklace like she wore in a photograph, but then you had a dream, and it told you your mother is still alive."

When she put it in such plain terms, it sounded like a tall tale.

"I know it sounds crazy, but I'm being honest," I said.

She looked back down at her notes. "And that man—Orson—lost his wife last night, and when you got to the parking lot, his car was gone."

"We saw them together as we were heading out onto the trail," I said. "They should have easily found the parking lot with the flashlight I gave them. But he said she found some mushrooms and made him eat one. Then, when they were almost to the parking lot, she screamed. He said he searched for her all night but got lost. In the morning, he came upon us in the cave."

"Then you almost ran him over?" Deb said.

"Unintentionally," I said. "And we didn't."

"Right," Deb said, closing her notebook. "I suppose the first thing we need to do is head into that cave and recover the body."

———

It took longer than I imagined it would to get to the cave. Deb had insisted we bring a paramedic, the coroner, and a couple of additional officers. To make matters worse, my ankle was still throbbing with every step. Xander had offered to take them so I could stay, but I had to see this through.

What if my dream was wrong, and that woman was my mother? As much as I wanted to believe my dream, it might have simply been a dream.

When we got to the stone staircase, I knew something was off.

"Hold on," I said. "These aren't our footprints."

Deb walked to the front of the group to look. "These look fresher, for sure."

"This cave isn't as remote as we thought it was," Xander said.

"It's still a bit early in the season for tourists," Deb said. "But maybe someone came out to avoid the mid-summer crowds."

There had been a few cars in the parking lot when we'd gotten back to the park. Maybe she was right.

"We'll go first," Deb said, motioning for one of her fellow officers to join her at the front of the pack. "Where's the body?"

"Down the cave, almost to the end, and to the left. Go into the crevice until you can't go any farther," I said.

Deb nodded. "Stay here until we tell you it's safe."

The rest of us stayed and waited, listening for even the slightest bit of noise.

It seemed like forever before Deb called out, "Come on back."

"I might stay and wait out here if that's okay?" Xander said.

"Sure," I said. "No problem."

He looked relieved not to have to go back into the cave.

I was the last person down because I was the slowest.

"Is this what you saw last night?" Deb asked when I got to the back of the cave.

The scene before me was grizzly. The bones that had once been part of a whole body were now scattered throughout the back of the cave and into the crevice.

I shined my light around, trying to see if it would reflect off the necklace. I had to find the necklace. If it was my mother, I wanted that necklace.

"What are you looking for?" Deb asked.

"The necklace," I said. "I didn't touch it last night because I knew it might have fingerprints or something on it, but I don't see it anywhere."

"Maybe it's back in the crevice," Deb said. "I'll help you look."

"I don't think I can get back there," I said. "I twisted my ankle last night."

"Then I'll look," Deb said. "But this isn't how you left it, right?"

"She was in one piece when I left last night," I said. "She was sitting toward the back of the crevice."

"Did you see anything else while you were back there?" Deb asked.

"I only had my headlamp, but other than what I told you at the station and the necklace, no."

"Can one of you escort Ellie back to the entrance of the cave?" Deb asked one of the officers. "I want you to go home. Ice and elevate your leg."

"But what if she—"

"We won't be able to determine who she was for several days. Maybe longer if the lab is backed up."

Patience was not one of my virtues, but I had no other choice. The pain was getting so bad it was radiating up my leg. A little voice in my head told me it was more than a sprain, but I pushed it away. Those thoughts would make it nearly impossible to get back to Mona.

"Did they find her?" Xander asked when I returned to the mouth of the cave.

I nodded. "But the necklace is missing, and the bones are scattered all over the place."

"Do you think an animal got to them?"

"After all this time?"

Xander shrugged. "Maybe we lured one in last night with the smell of the delicious soup."

"It was from a can—I can give you a couple when we get home. I mean, to my house." Apparently, I wasn't in too much pain to blush.

"I knew what you meant," Xander said, helping me up the stairs.

The walk back to the car was excruciatingly slow. I kept tripping over things, which made my ankle feel even worse.

"Whoa, careful," Xander said, grabbing my wrist. "That's where that cliff is, remember?"

My scalp tingled. The cliff.

"Hold on to my arm." I held my arm out for Xander to grab. He didn't.

"Why?"

"Just hold on to it," I said. "I want to peek out over the cliff."

"No." He crossed his arms over his chest.

"I'm going to do it whether you hold on to me or not."

Xander reluctantly reached out and took my hand.

"Don't let go," I said with a smile.

"You can bet your life I won't."

"Isn't that exactly what I'm doing?"

He laughed.

I took a step closer to the edge. I had to push a couple of tree branches out of the way, but the feeling in my scalp told me all I needed to know before my eyes could confirm.

There was a body at the bottom of the cliff.

"You can pull me back up," I said.

Xander pulled, and my ankle twisted again, causing me to let go of his hand.

Thankfully, he didn't let go of mine.

When I was back upright, I crumbled to the ground.

"Ellie, what's wrong?"

The pain was so excruciating, I couldn't speak. If my ankle hadn't been broken before, it was now.

"Talk to me. Are you okay? What was down there?"

I gritted my teeth and looked up at him. "Body down there." I sucked in a breath. "And my ankle is broken."

Xander crouched down next to me. "Can you heal it?"

I didn't have any idea what he was talking about.

"You know what I mean," Xander said. "You heal people all the time. But can you heal yourself?"

Did my magic work that way?

I'd only know if I tried.

My hands were already wrapped around my ankle. I

closed my eyes and focused all the energy and magic I had into it, but if anything, the pain became worse.

I shook my head. "Can you?"

"My magic doesn't work that way." Xander's voice cracked.

"Someone else?"

Xander thought about this for a moment. "The Grand Witch. But our phones are dead. Why didn't we recharge them?" He grunted in frustration.

"Go get the paramedic," I said through my gritted teeth.

"Yes," Xander said, jumping to his feet. "Will you be okay?"

"Just hurry." The tears pooling in my eyes gave away just how much pain I was in.

"I will."

We'd been to the cave enough to know the way by now. I wasn't worried about him getting lost. At least not until I'd been sitting there for what felt like well over an hour.

I was getting light-headed, and my ankle was swelling larger by the minute. I needed to elevate it.

I laid in the mud and propped my ankle onto a large rock at the edge of the cliff. From this vantage point, I could see the person lying there. It looked a lot like Jerri— Orson's wife, but I couldn't be sure since I'd only seen her for a few seconds by the light of a flashlight.

Consciousness was becoming harder and harder to hold on to. Now and again, I thought I heard Xander's voice, but then no one came.

My last memory was of a bloody finger hidden under a

bush.

When I woke up, I was lying in a hospital bed.

"Where am I?" I asked a nurse who was quietly typing away on a mobile computer station.

"You're in Iowa City at the hospital," she said sweetly. "You broke your ankle."

"How did I get here?"

"The Cliff Haven ambulance brought you."

"Is she awake?" Xander's voice came through the door before his body did. Or maybe they'd just given me too much medication to know the difference.

"She'll be groggy for a while," the nurse said. "Let her rest."

Xander was at my side in a flash, his hands cupping mine. "I thought you were gone. I found you lying there. It's a good thing you didn't roll over, or you would have ended up the same way Jerri did."

"It was Jerri?" I asked, then blackness overtook the light.

When I opened my eyes again, the overhead lights were dimmed, and someone was snoring softly next to me.

Every part of my body was heavy. My head felt like a boulder when I tried to turn it to see who was there.

I expected to find Xander but found Jake instead. I turned my head the other way, but no one else was in the room.

Was I dreaming? Or had Jake come back from his engagement celebration trip to be at my bedside?

The next time I woke up, the sun shone through the window, and a whole gaggle of people surrounded my bed.

K atie's face lit up with joy when she realized I was awake. Earl, Hank, Nancy, Fran, Bonnie, Amy, Xander, Jake, Deb, and several other people were there. Noticeably missing were Georgia, Bex, and Laura. Though Bex and Laura probably hadn't heard about me being in the hospital.

"Hi," I croaked out. My throat felt like I'd eaten a bowl of hot desert sand.

Katie handed me the standard-issue hospital water bottle, complete with a thick plastic bendy straw. I took a sip and cleared my throat. "Thanks."

"How are you feeling, kiddo?" Earl asked.

"Tired," I said. "But not in pain anymore."

"Good," a doctor said, making her way through the visitors. "Typically, we don't allow this many people in a room, but they all claim to be family."

I smiled. "They are."

"So be it," the doctor said. "Your x-rays show that you've broken the ankle in several places. We'll have to do surgery, and you'll have a long recovery, but you will walk again."

"That's good to hear," I said. "Do I have to stay here, or can I go home?"

"As long as someone drives you home and promises to stay with you, there's no need for you to stay here. We'll get you all splinted and stabilized, but we'll want you back just as soon as the orthopedic surgeon can get you in."

The doctor lifted the bottom of the sheet to look at my ankle one last time. It was so ugly—black, blue, and swollen—a few people in the room turned away. "Keep it elevated and use crutches when you need to get around. But only move around when necessary."

That was like telling a polar bear he had to live in the rainforest. "I'll do my best."

"The nurse will be in to discharge you soon." She left, and everyone started talking at once about who would stay with me and how they'd take shifts cooking.

They seemed to have everything figured out by the time the nurse came back with the discharge papers.

"I'll drive her home," Jake said, and nobody argued.

"I'll bring Mona," Xander said with a smile.

Jake wheeled me out to his truck and lifted me into the passenger seat.

"Where's Georgia?" I asked when he got into the driver's side.

"She had to get some work done," Jake said. "She'll stop over later tonight if that's okay."

"Sorry you had to come back so soon. I would have understood if you hadn't."

"Between you and a potential double homicide, I had no choice."

"And Georgia was okay with that?" My medication was making my tongue looser than normal, but I didn't mind. It would be good to know.

"Not really," he said. "You know how I told you she and I had been working on me leaving work at work."

"Yeah, that's stupid." I clapped a hand over my mouth. Maybe a loose tongue wasn't the best idea.

Jake laughed. "Tell me how you really feel."

"I feel like you abandoned my mother." Loose tongues were definitely not the best.

Jake looked over at me and frowned. "I didn't expect that."

I literally bit my tongue. There would be nothing good to come from my emotional outbursts. And right now, my emotions were all over the place. My hair was probably changing from straight to frizzy, white to pink to orange to yellow.

"I never meant to abandon Emily," Jake said. "I'm as surprised as you are that I fell for Georgia—especially because she's a witch. Not that there's anything wrong with witches," he added quickly. "But I thought Emily would be the only one I'd ever love."

I could almost taste the blood I was biting down so hard. But I couldn't let my feelings loose. Not when I had absolutely no filter.

Jake glanced over at me, then back at the road. "I'll tell you one thing, though. I will never abandon you."

My vision was fuzzy with the tears in my eyes.

"I know you're not biologically mine," Jake said. "But

sometimes I feel like you're my daughter. And if I'd have met you when you were a child, I would have adopted you in a heartbeat."

"I wish you were my dad," I said, my tongue no longer held captive by my pearly whites.

"I do, too," Jake said. "And I know you're only speaking so freely because of this medication, but I'm pleased we can talk about this."

I wiped a tear from my eye. I was too.

"Now, what do you think about Georgia?" Jake lifted an eyebrow. "Be honest."

"She's really pretty and super nice, and I want you to be happy."

"But . . ?"

"She's not Emily."

"No, she most definitely is not."

"Do you think the woman I found in the cave is—was —Emily?"

Jake shook his head. "There's no way of knowing."

"In the photo Harriet gave me—the one taken right after I was born—Emily is wearing a necklace. Do you remember it?"

"I think it was her class necklace," Jake said. "A gold circle with an etching of a flower on the front?"

"That's it," I said. "The woman I found in the cave was wearing the same necklace."

"Is that why you think it's her?"

"It makes sense."

"It would make sense if you didn't grow up here."

"What do you mean?"

"They give those necklaces to every young woman who

graduates Cliff Haven High. The young men get cufflinks. It's a tradition. The necklaces haven't changed in half a century. My mother's necklace was identical to Emily's."

I slumped a bit. "Well, that's just fantastic."

"Except for one thing," Jake said with a smile as if he was ready to reveal who the grand prize winner was.

He paused.

"What's the one thing?" I asked out of pure necessity.

"The necklaces and cufflinks are engraved. The necklaces have the recipient's initials on the opposite side of the flower."

"Meaning, if we found the necklace, we'd be able to figure out who it belonged to?"

"Or at least narrow it down based on the initials."

Excitement rose in my chest. "Do you know if Deb found the necklace?"

Jake shook his head. "I don't think they had yet, but they're still out there trying to recover all the bones."

"Do they know what happened with the bones? Was it an animal?"

"Preliminary assessment is that it wasn't," Jake said. "It looks like a human did it."

"Messing with a dead body? Why would someone do that?"

"Maybe they realized someone was onto them."

"The killer?"

Jake nodded. "*If* she was killed, that is. We have to wait until all the bones are back together for the coroner to give us the official report."

We sat in silence for a few minutes as my mind raced through all the possibilities. If we found the necklace, we could know for sure who it was. It could be Melly May, though I was reasonably confident I'd tracked her magic, and that wouldn't have been possible if she was dead. But if she was alive, why was she hiding? And visiting a corpse? Or had someone else had the ring on more recently than Melly May? Maybe I had been tracking another witch or warlock's magic.

Was Orson responsible for both of the women's deaths? Maybe he killed the woman in the cave years before and brought Jerri out there to kill her the same way. Heck, who knew how many bodies we'd find if we investigated every crevice in those caves. Maybe he'd killed far more than two women.

And what if the woman he'd killed—the one I'd found —was Emily? I gulped down the bile rising in my throat. Just the thought of her being dead made me want to vomit.

"What if Emily's alive and comes back and you're married to Georgia?"

For a moment, I thought maybe I'd only considered the question in my head. I certainly hadn't wanted it to escape my lips. But I was pretty sure I'd said the words aloud.

"I don't know," Jake finally whispered.

He didn't know? How could he not know? He either loved Emily, or he loved Georgia. You couldn't love two people at the same time. Not like that. Not in a way that made you want to marry them both.

"You don't know?" I asked. "How is that possible? You have to know."

"The odds that Emily will come back are slim."

"Does that mean you're giving up on finding her? Didn't you tell me you'd never stop looking?"

Jake turned off the interstate and stopped at the stop sign at the end of the off-ramp. "I won't ever stop looking for her." He turned down the highway toward my house. "But if—when—I marry Georgia, I'll be looking for Emily for your sake, not for mine anymore."

Tears stung at my eyes. I was tired of crying, but the medication seemed to loosen my tear ducts in addition to my tongue. It made me happy that he wouldn't stop looking for Emily, but I couldn't imagine how she would feel if she did come back and found out that Jake was married.

Jake turned into my driveway behind Xander and Mona and put his truck in park but didn't turn it off. "I don't mean for this to come off harsh, but there's no other way to say it."

I looked up at him.

"Emily abandoned both of us a long time ago." His voice was gentle, but his words stung. "We don't owe her anything. In fact, it should be the other way around."

He was right. I'd often felt that way but never had the nerve to say it aloud.

"But if we find her," he continued, "I'll be happy to be her friend. And no matter what, I always want to be part of your life."

I nodded.

Xander opened my door. "I'll carry you inside." He lifted me from the seat gently, as if I would break if he moved too quickly. I wrapped my arms around his neck and resisted the urge to put my head on his shoulder. I might have been on medication, but I still didn't want to be his rebound.

Jake opened the front door and turned on the lights.

Xander carried me upstairs to my bedroom. "Renée will be by later to drop off Penelope and see what she can do about your ankle."

I'd completely forgotten about the possibility of Renée

healing me. "Don't you think the doctor will be suspicious if I come back and everything is healed?"

"So don't go back."

"Won't that look even worse?"

"They have so many patients. They probably won't even notice."

That wasn't reassuring at all. "We'll see."

Xander gently lowered me into my bed and covered me with the quilt that always smelled like lavender—the way I imagined my grandmother smelled when she was alive.

"You can't possibly think it would be better to stay in pain when there are other options."

My mind probably wasn't thinking rationally, but the thought of the doctors knowing how my bones had magically healed seemed pretty dangerous.

"Jake is bringing you some food and ice," Xander said. "But before he comes up, can I give you a quick kiss?"

"We can't just be kissing," I said. "I like you. A lot. Like way more than I should. But you friend-zoned me, started dating my arch-nemesis, were upset when she broke up with you, then kissed me in a way I want to be kissed every day for the rest of my life, but I can't. Because we're friends. And Penelope would bite you."

"Knock knock," Jake said in the doorway.

"Did you hear all of that?" I asked.

"Just the end," Jake said. "But it's not my business."

Xander looked like he was in shock.

Jake slapped him on the back. "It's the medication. It turned off her filter."

Xander nodded, and Jake laughed.

"Speaking of medication," I said. "When am I supposed to take more?"

"Are you in pain?" Jake asked as he and Xander both jumped into action, lifting my ankle and applying the ice.

I chuckled. "Not yet, but I'm sure it'll wear off soon, and I want to be prepared."

"You can take more now," Jake said, looking over the discharge papers to make sure. "It's probably best to stay on top of the pain. Do you want me to get it for you?"

"That would be great," I said. "Thank you."

When Jake left, Xander sat on the edge of my bed.

"Sorry about my lack of filter," I said.

"I had no idea you felt so . . . strongly."

"About what?"

Xander looked at me. "About me. About us. About Laura."

"It's probably because you're the first warlock I've ever met." I nudged his shoulder. "Don't warlocks have some sort of special seduction powers?"

"I wish," Xander said, then wrinkled his nose. "That wasn't what I meant."

"It's okay. I'm not offended."

"So, where does that leave us?" Xander asked.

"I don't know." I shifted to make more room for him. "But we should probably talk about it when I'm not practically high."

"That sounds like a good idea."

The sound of a piggy squealing was like music to my ears.

She charged up the stairs and burst through my bedroom door.

Xander lifted her up onto the bed, and she started doing circles, falling all over herself.

"I'm happy to see you too, sweetheart." I grabbed her and pulled her wiggly body into my chest.

Tears once again moistened my cheeks. Penelope gave me cute little nose kisses, then started investigating every bit of me.

"It's my ankle," I said. "It's broken."

"We'll see about that," Renée said.

Xander stood and bowed his head at her.

"That's unnecessary," she said. "But thank you."

Maybe it was because I hadn't grown up in the magical world, but it was hard to see her as anything but my friend Renée, who had needed help lifting her baggage.

"Thank you for bringing Penelope," I said. "I hope she was good for you."

"She was the perfect house guest," Renée said. "You're lucky to have one another."

"You can say that again," I said.

"You're lucky to have one another." Renée laughed at her joke. "Now, stay still. This shouldn't take but a moment."

"Wait," I said when she reached for my leg. "I'm not sure I want you to heal it."

Renée let out a burst of laughter. "You're joking, right? Aren't you in pain?"

"I'm sure I will be when the medicine wears off, but what will the doctors think when I just show up with my leg magically healed? What will the town think?"

"They'll think you're a witch and had a witch friend magically heal you." Renée's voice was firm.

"But if people know you could heal me, don't you think they'll be coming to you constantly trying to get healing too?"

"They won't because you won't tell them who healed you," she said. "You could even call it a miracle if you wanted to."

"But that would be a lie. And it would cheapen the idea of actual miracles."

Renée looked like she understood my point but was frustrated with me nonetheless. "It's completely up to you, but I feel you'd be making a mistake in not taking the healing."

"Can you come back tomorrow when my head is on straighter? I don't want to decide while I'm on medication."

Xander laughed. "You'll have a lot to think about when you're off the medication."

Renée looked at Xander, then back at me as if she had no idea what he was talking about, but didn't much care either. "That makes perfect sense to me," Renée said. "But call me in the middle of the night if the pain gets overwhelming. I don't sleep well, anyway. I'm more of a daytime napper."

She leaned over and hugged me. "I'm so glad you're okay. And once you're all better, we'll have to go dancing."

"Sounds like a plan," I said.

When she stood, she said, "One last thing, did you find Melly May?"

"I followed Melly May's trail, or at least what I assumed was her trail if she was truly the last one to wear the ring."

Renée nodded. "It could have been someone else, I suppose."

"The trail led us directly to a partially decomposed body," I said. "The body had been there for a while. As in years. But I wouldn't have been able to follow a trail of someone if they'd been dead for years, would I?"

Renée thought about this. "I don't know the extent of your magic, but I would guess not."

"I would, too," I said. "Especially since the trail weakened as time went on."

"So either Melly May is still alive," Renée said. "Or someone else wore the ring recently."

"Basically, yes."

"That's good to know. I'll pass the information along to Lucy."

"Can you wait until I can go with you?" I asked. "I'd like to be there when you talk to her."

"You'd be able to visit her sooner if I just fixed that ankle of yours. Plus, just think of all the money you'll save not having to go through surgery." Renée gave me a sly smile. "Still no?"

I laughed and shook my head. "Maybe tomorrow."

"If I don't hear from you by nine, I'll be at your doorstep," she said, walking toward the door.

"Make it ten," I said.

"Ten it is."

Jake walked in as she walked out. "Everything seems to be good here. Penelope looks happy to be home." He handed me a pain pill and a glass of water.

Penelope was fast asleep next to my ankle, her breaths coming out in little snores.

"I think I'll try to sleep." I yawned and handed the glass back to him. "I'm pretty worn out."

"Jake and I will both be here tonight," Xander said.

"Georgia got called away for a story, so she won't make it." Jake gave me an apologetic look.

"No problem," I said. "Sleep in whichever room will allow it."

They both nodded. They knew the house's quirks and how only certain rooms allowed certain people to sleep in them.

"If you need anything, you can just yell," Xander said. "Or call on your cell."

"Where is my cell?" I asked, looking around. Usually, I charged it in the kitchen at night.

"I must have left it downstairs," Xander said. "I'll be right back."

"You got everything you need?" Jake asked.

"I think so," I said. "Thank you for staying. You don't have to."

"Doctor's orders," he said. "And for the record, I'd be okay if you wanted to kiss Xander again."

Penelope perked up when he said this and looked up at me.

"Don't worry," I said to her. "We won't be doing any kissing. Not for a while."

She didn't look appeased.

"What crawled up her bonnet?" Jake asked.

"She doesn't think Xander and I should be together." I shrugged. "She's never warned me off a guy before. Even the bad ones." I sat up and scratched her behind the ear. "You're adorable, but I think your good-guy radar is a bit off."

When Xander walked in holding my phone and the charging cord, Penelope stared him down.

"You told her, didn't you?" he asked.

"That we kissed?" I laughed. "Yes, she knows."

"I guess it's a plus she's not attacking me right now." Xander searched for an outlet behind my bed and left my phone charging on the nightstand. "There, now you can call one of us if you need anything."

Penelope was still staring right at him.

"Goodnight," he said, hurrying to the door. "I'll see you in the morning."

"He seems so tough until it comes to a little piggy," I said.

Jake walked toward the door. "I think he has the right idea. That little piggy is more than she seems."

He turned off the light and closed the door.

"Goodnight, Penelope," I said. "I love you so much."

She nuzzled into me.

I stared at the ceiling for quite some time before fading off into a deep sleep.

The medication didn't only make me loose-lipped during the day, it also gave me the strangest dreams.

First, I was skydiving off the back of an eagle into a pool made entirely of blue gelatin. Then, I was in a cave with a disco ball and pink dancing giraffes. But the last one was the strangest and most vivid.

I was walking through the state park. The trails seemed normal, but the plants were all scorched like they'd just gone through a fire. The trees bent over as if they were sad. And a strange house appeared in front of me.

Boards crisscrossed over the entrance but were easy to duck under.

The inside was made of marshmallows—toasted ones —and the longer I stayed inside, the more toasted they became until they started charring and lighting on fire.

I turned to get back out, but my ankle was stuck. And it hurt.

Then the image of a woman appeared in the doorway and reached out a hand.

I took it without a second thought. It was that or burn alive.

She took me to the basement of the house, accessed from the outside. A charred board was off to the side.

The basement was cool and showed no indication that the house was burning above us.

I sat on a pillow in the middle of the room, and she put her hands on my ankle.

In an instant, the pain subsided.

I exhaled.

"Thank you," I said, my words coming out as if I had a handful of marbles in my mouth.

But she seemed to understand. And when she looked up at me, I gasped.

My eyes flew open to find darkness still surrounding me.

But I wasn't in my bed. In fact, I was on my feet.

I reached around to find a light switch, but when my fingers came in contact with the wall—it wasn't the wall of my bedroom. My fingertips touched cool stone.

My chest tightened. Where was I?

I needed to use my magic to light the surrounding space. Closing my eyes, I saw the woman again.

A young Esme stood smiling at me.

I opened my eyes, expecting to see her in front of me. Maybe she was a ghost. A magical, ankle-healing ghost.

Find the edges of magic.

The darkness was all-encompassing, but finally, I found a sparkle—a tiny shimmer in the darkness. When I latched onto it, the room brightened and came into focus.

I was in the basement.

Alone.

I bent down to examine my ankle. How had I gotten down here alone on a broken ankle? At first, I thought maybe the pain medication had just kicked in. But the sensation wasn't numbness from the ice or dulling of the pain from medicine. It was as if the pain was completely gone.

There was no swelling.

The bones felt normal.

"Renée? Are you in here? Did you heal me without my consent?"

Maybe I was still dreaming.

I looked around at the basement. Since I'd found it beneath my kitchen island, I'd been intimidated by it. This was Esme's study. Books and writings and desks and artifacts coexisted as if I was amid some sort of museum curated by my magical grandmother. Most of the books and writings were in languages I didn't understand. But being down here made me feel inferior. Like I didn't know my magic well enough to be in the presence of such magical things.

I slipped into one of the chairs at a desk that had papers strewn about. I hadn't had it in me to organize the office. It would feel wrong to disturb what Esme had going on.

But then a heading on a piece of paper caught my attention. I gently slipped it out from beneath the others, trying to memorize where I'd gotten it so I could slip it back into the same spot when I was finished.

Melly May Blake
 Evidence: Finger
 Magical Tracking: Ineffective
 Feelings: Misty has an alibi, but something is off. She

won't talk about it, and the police won't press her for details because of said alibi.

Conclusions: Deceased – Body missing – Cause unknown

As I glanced at the other papers on the table, they all had a similar format. These were Esme's case notes. Some were more detailed than others with far more feelings and evidence, while others simply had a name at the top.

I slipped the piece back where it had been and headed back up the stairs. I needed to talk to Misty about her sister's disappearance.

21

"Rise and shine, sleepyhead," Renée said as she opened the curtains in my bedroom, letting in a stream of bright sunshine. "We couldn't wait any longer for you to wake up."

"What time is it?" I asked, my throat dry.

"It's almost noon," Katie said, bustling in with a tray of breakfast and coffee.

"Noon?" I hardly ever slept in. The medicine must have completely taken me out. Except for my moment of sleepwalking. The memory of what I'd found in the basement flooded back to my mind.

"I'm guessing you need some of these." Nancy—in her red velour jogging outfit—handed me a couple of pills and a glass of water.

I took them from her, but before I put them in my mouth, I shifted my ankle to find there wasn't any pain.

I handed her back the pills and reached for my ankle.

"I don't think you should do that," Nancy said, worry in her voice.

I pulled back the blankets to find my ankle, looking exactly as it had before I'd hurt it.

Katie gasped. "How in the world?"

I peeked over at Renée, but she looked just as shocked as Katie. She shook her head, telling me she wasn't responsible.

"It's a doggone miracle," Fran said.

Every single person in the room turned and stared at me.

"Okay, you're messing with us, right," Amy said. "Because there's no way—"

I swung my legs to the floor and stood.

Amy's eyes widened. Katie looked like she might pass out.

"This will sound crazy," I said. "But I think Esme healed it."

Everyone but Renée laughed.

"How would Esme have healed it?" Renée asked, her voice serious as she approached my bed. "Is she alive?"

"Of course, she's not," Fran said. "We were at the funeral. Saw her lying in that box. Those meds are probably just better than Ellie's giving them credit for."

I jumped up and down. "My ankle is perfectly fine. And I don't feel medicated at all anymore." A rush of memories flooded back. All the things I'd said to Xander and Jake. "Oh no."

"That's what I thought," Fran said. "You probably went and broke it worse."

I shook my head and plopped back down on the bed. "It's not the ankle. I'll never be able to show my face around Jake and Xander again."

Amy's face widened into a smile. "Yeah, we heard."

Fran nudged her in the ribs but couldn't hide her own smile.

"Looks like I'm never leaving this bedroom." I laid back and pulled the covers over my head.

"Jake and Xander both had to leave earlier this morning," Katie said. "You can come out."

"Nope," I said. "Not coming out."

"Don't be ridiculous," Renée said, pulling the blanket off me. "Get up so we can solve this case."

"There's nothing to solve yet," I said. "They still have to get the bones put together."

"I suspect they're about done with that." She glanced at my phone the second it buzzed.

I reached over to find Jake's name on the screen. I glanced at Renée, who shrugged. "Are you going to answer it or let it go to voicemail?"

"Hello?" I said into the receiver.

"Hey, how are you feeling?" Jake asked.

"Better than I could have ever imagined possible," I said.

"That's great news."

"What's up?"

The women surrounding me looked like they might topple over if they leaned any farther forward.

"We got the bones back together. We didn't find the necklace, though. If you're up for it, could you come down to the coroner's office and see if you get any feelings off either Jerri's body or Melly May's?"

I'd never been asked to use my feelings on a dead body

before. Esme had powerful feelings when it came to solving crimes, but mine were still developing.

"I can be there in fifteen minutes," I said.

Everyone in the room gaped at me.

"Don't overdo it," Jake said. "We'll be here whenever you can make it."

"Really," I said. "I think either the doctors got it wrong, or I was miraculously healed because I feel like my normal self."

Jake was quiet on the other end of the line.

"You still there?" I asked.

"Sorry, yeah," he said. "Just distracted. I'll see you in a bit."

He disconnected before I could say goodbye. It was probably a lot for him to comprehend that my ankle—which looked disastrous yesterday—was now all better.

"Looks like you're right," I said to Renée. "Jake wants me to come down and see if I can get any feelings off the bodies."

Renée nodded.

"No way," Katie said. "He should know better than to ask this of you. You were in the hospital less than twenty-four hours ago. You need your rest."

"Being as it's almost noon," I said with a smile, "I think I got plenty of rest last night."

"Are you certain you're okay?" Nancy asked.

"Pretty certain," I said. "But I appreciate your concern. Honestly, it feels nice to be doted on."

"If you'd like me to check it out, I can," Renée said. "Just to be sure."

"Are you a doctor all of a sudden?" Amy asked.

I laughed and glanced at Renée. "Can I tell them?"

"Go right ahead."

"Renée is a witch like me," I said. "But more like the queen of the witches."

"You give me entirely too much credit," Renée said. "It's like the President only in the magical community."

"The President of the magical community lives in Cliff Haven, Iowa?" Fran laughed. "Yeah, sure."

"I've known you your entire life," Nancy said. "And I had no idea you were a witch."

"Most people don't," Renée said. "After I saw the ridicule Esme had to deal with, I didn't want to go through the same thing. But now, Cliff Haven and its residents—especially Ellie's friends—seem to be much more welcoming. It's not necessarily something I want the entire town to know. Though, if they do, it's okay."

Everyone contemplated this in silence until Renée said, "So how about I check out that ankle so we can get you over to the police station?"

"And you're sure you saw Esme in your dream?" Renée asked as she drove me to the police station. She'd done her magic but said the ankle was healed entirely before her touch.

"She was younger," I said. "But, yes, it was Esme. I have lots of pictures of her around the house."

"It's a beautiful home," Renée said. "Full of magic."

I smiled. "I am so thankful for the gift she gave me. I wish I could have met her."

"It appears your wish may have come true. If only in your dreams."

I'd take Esme in my dreams over no Esme at all.

"After you finish up here, I'll drive you over to Sunny Meadows so we can tell Lucy about your expedition." Renée turned into the police station parking lot.

"And maybe I'll have more information after talking to the coroner."

"Let's hope we can bring her some closure," Renée said. "Poor Misty has been a wreck since it happened."

"Speaking of Misty," I said. "I'd like to talk to her if that's possible."

"From what I've heard, she's not doing very well with everything going on. She's been drunk most of the time since the ring was found."

"I'd still like to talk to her," I said. "She seemed perfectly okay when I worked with her on another case."

"She puts on a good front, but she struggled a lot in life. Being in Melly May's shadow probably didn't help."

I opened the door and stepped gently onto my ankle in case it really had been the medicine that made it better, but it was still perfectly okay. "Thanks for the ride."

"I'll be here when you get finished."

I walked into the police station, and the receptionist took me down a staircase to the basement. I'd been in various sections of the police station but never in the basement. Whether the temperature was as cold as the cave or I was sensing something, chills ran sprints all over my body.

"Ellie," a tiny woman, probably in her mid-forties,

with long twists and thick glasses, greeted me. "I'm Neve, the coroner."

"It's nice to meet you." I tried to focus on her instead of the two bodies lying on metal tables next to her. At least they were covered with white sheets.

"First thing's first, if you ever start to feel light-headed, I want you to sit down, put your head between your knees, and take deep breaths in and out of your mouth. Dead bodies can have strange effects on people."

I nodded.

"And second, all of my findings are preliminary and cannot be shared outside these walls. With anyone."

I hesitated. Renée was the Grand Witch. Was I obligated to tell her whatever I knew?

"This might be the only place in Cliff Haven that can keep a secret," Neve said. "Can you?"

"Yes," I said. "I won't say anything." I might be a witch, but I didn't know the laws of the magical world. Renée couldn't possibly expect me to divulge everything.

Neve looked satisfied with my answer and pulled the sheet back from the first body—Jerri. "This one is pretty straightforward," she said. "She fell off a cliff and broke her neck. She likely died on impact."

The scream we'd heard was her falling. "So, there was nothing we could have done for her if we'd been there right after she fell?"

"It's doubtful anyone could have saved her." Neve started to put the sheet back over Jerri's body, but I stopped her.

"What about her hands?" I asked.

Neve's face lit up. "Did you get a feeling? I used to

love working with your grandmother. She was always so intuitive."

I didn't have the heart to tell her this didn't come from a feeling but genuine curiosity. "Something like that."

"Like Esme's were, your feelings are dead on." She lifted one of the hands. "Under her nails was DNA from someone she probably tried to use to keep her on the cliff. And do you see her fingertips, how they're practically destroyed? That's because she probably tried to grab onto the cliff as she fell or had hold of it before she fell. This woman did not go down without a fight." The way Neve said it and how she looked at Jerri, she seemed proud.

I smiled. Even though it wasn't easy for me to be amongst dead bodies, it was cool to see people excited about their jobs.

"What about the other hand?" I asked.

Neve smiled even bigger. "I wondered if you'd ask."

She seemed to be testing my abilities. Thankfully, I'd seen the finger because I probably wouldn't have even thought to ask. Doubt filled me. What if I didn't have the same abilities as Esme? Would Neve not want to work with me anymore?

Neve moved to the other side of the bed and lifted the sheet. "Is this what you sensed?"

Jerri's left hand was missing its ring finger.

22

"I have to be honest with you." I took a deep breath. "I didn't sense her missing finger or anything underneath her fingernails. I knew she would be missing a finger because I saw it when I was lying on the edge of the cliff."

Neve's smile faltered a bit. "Are you saying you don't have the same abilities as Esme did?"

"I-I don't know." I looked down at my shoes.

"She does," Jake said, walking into the room. "She just has to believe in them."

He wrapped an arm around my shoulder, and all the embarrassing things I'd said the night before came rushing back to me.

"Do your hair colors mean the same as Esme's did?" Neve asked.

I pulled a strand of hair forward and examined it. It was a light blue verging on purple and in tight spirals.

"What would this have meant for Esme?" I asked.

"Embarrassment or maybe unease," Neve said. "But

you don't need to be embarrassed by your abilities—regardless of how strong they are."

"Or by the words you say when you're being honest." Jake squeezed my shoulder and then dropped his hand down so he could open a file to show me a photo of a wrecked car. "We found Orson's car this morning in a ditch. It looks like someone stole it after all and then crashed it before running away."

"Is there any evidence indicating who stole it?" I asked.

"Not yet, but we're still looking." Jake closed the file. "I was hoping you could join me at the site to see if you had any feelings." He looked down at my leg. "That is if you're truly feeling up to it."

"We should probably pick up the finger too," I said.

"The finger?" Jake asked.

"Jerri's," I said. "I think I saw it when I was on the edge of the cliff."

Jake nodded. "Are you all finished here?"

"Not quite," Neve said. "We haven't gotten to the main event yet."

She seemed giddy.

Jake grinned but wrinkled his nose a bit. He obviously felt the same way about being around dead bodies as I did. "I'll wait for you upstairs."

"I don't want you to feel pressured," Neve said when Jake was gone. "We have lots of evidence being processed to help find out who this person was, but I wanted to give you the opportunity."

She moved to the second table with the white draping.

Even without lifting it, it was apparent there was far less underneath.

"Are you still feeling okay?" Neve asked. "You're not going to pass out on me, are you?"

"I'm doing all right," I said.

"Good." She carefully lifted the sheet to reveal the woman I'd seen in the cave, only pieced together like a skeletal jigsaw puzzle. "This is the most fascinating thing I've ever seen."

"Why is that?" I asked.

"I've done some research since we live so close to caves but have never seen a body that has been in a cave before. She may have been in there for decades. Do you see how there's still hair? And some skin?"

I watched as she pointed to the places where a thin strip of skin was still covering the bone. My stomach contracted a bit, but I wouldn't let myself throw up. This was important. Especially to Lucy.

Crap.

I was supposed to go with Renée to see Lucy, but I just told Jake I'd go with him to look at the car and find the finger.

"You still okay?" Neve interrupted my thoughts.

"Sorry," I said. "I realized I double-booked myself this afternoon."

"Sucks," she said. "But like I was saying, this body is one of a kind."

I tried to pull myself back to the task at hand. I'd fix my double-booking problem later. Right now, I needed to see if I got any feelings or inclinations about this body.

Especially since there was still a possibility that it was my mother.

My stomach tightened again. I sucked in a breath and could almost taste the smell of rotting flesh. I gagged.

"Do you need to sit down?" Neve said.

I shook my head. "Keep going."

She eyed me suspiciously but turned back to the body. "I would hypothesize she's been there at least five to ten years, but with the cave's environment, that may be incorrect." She glanced back up at me. "Do you think you can try to get a feeling, or will you throw up on the body? Because I don't want to take the chance if you're going to barf on her. She doesn't need that after all she's been through."

"I think I'll be okay." I took a step forward and concentrated. "Didn't someone find Melly May's finger? Is this woman missing a finger?"

"She is," Neve said, but her voice was hesitant. "We can't say for certain it's her until we get a DNA match because, with how spread out her bones were, we may have simply missed it."

"Did you find all the other fingers?"

"We did."

I'd say that would be plenty of evidence to conclude this was Melly May, but I understood the professional aspect of not making assumptions.

"Which finger is she missing?"

"Her right pinky."

So not the same finger Jerri was missing. "Do you think the same person could have killed them?"

"That's not for me to decide," she said with a shrug. "I

leave that work to Jake and the others. And you, I suppose."

We stood there in silence while I tried to figure out something—anything—that might have told me who she was. A niggling feeling inside me said she wasn't Melly May, but that was probably because I'd assumed she had been the last one to wear the ring and the one who I'd tracked to the body. Finally, I shook my head. "I'm sorry, I'm not getting any feelings."

Neve was obviously disappointed, which made me feel terrible. For some reason, I desperately wanted to impress her. Maybe it was because she was way cooler than a lot of the people in Cliff Haven. Or maybe it was more because I wanted to prove myself.

"I'm sure Jake is waiting," Neve said.

I took this as her polite way of saying we were done. "Thanks for showing me all of this."

"I'm glad you stopped by," she said. "I'm sure we'll work together again in the future."

When I was back in the elevator, I inhaled deeply, trying to clear the dead body smell from my nose. When the doors opened on the main level, Jake stood waiting. "Did you figure it out?"

"Not yet," I said. "But maybe I will when we get to the car."

Jake nodded.

"The only thing is, I already promised to do something today," I said. "But can I meet you at the car's location?"

"That works," Jake said. "Do you mind if I have Deb pick up the finger?"

"Not at all," I said. "I'm perfectly okay seeing no more dead body parts for a while."

Jake laughed.

"Oh, and did anyone find the necklace?" I asked.

Jake shook his head. "Not yet. But we're still looking."

"Send me the location of the car," I said. "I'll text you when I'm on my way there."

"Took you long enough," Renée said when I got into her car. "Figure anything out?"

I remembered the warning Neve had given me. Not that there was anything to tell at this point. I suspected Neve thought I was going to solve the case right then and there.

But I hadn't.

I shook my head. "Nothing really."

"Have they at least figured out that it was Melly May?"

"No, and I'm starting to doubt that myself."

Renée looked over at me, and the car swerved to the right.

"Whoa," I said. "Keep your eyes on the road."

Renée corrected the car's course but didn't laugh. "We can't just walk into Sunny Meadows and tell Lucy we're back at square one."

"But we are," I said.

"What about the ring? And the tracking?"

"I know little about how my tracking works," I said.

"But from what I can tell, it doesn't track dead people."

I stopped. What if it did track dead people and what I'd seen of my mother was actually her being dead?

No.

It couldn't be because my tracking only tracked magic. People couldn't still have magic when they were dead.

Right?

"What are you thinking over there?"

"I was contemplating whether my magic could track someone who is dead. And hypothetically, it wouldn't because magic goes away when you die, right?"

"From what we can tell, yes. But I've never died, so it's hard to be certain." She winked at me.

"But then I thought, how would Esme have healed me since she's dead?"

"With magic," Renée said.

"Exactly. So if she healed me with magic and she's dead, then maybe I had been tracking Melly May."

"You're missing something," Renée said.

"I am?"

"You weren't tracking anyone's actual magic," she said. "You were tracking whoever last had the ring on."

"But the trail faded after a while, which would mean that the person had to have been there recently. And magical."

Renée thought about this for a minute. "You're right," she said. "If the trail faded, that would mean it has a time-stamp on it. And the person who last wore the ring was magical. And if that person was Melly May, she was either alive, or you were following a ghost with magic."

"That is completely unhelpful." I groaned in frustration.

"Don't let it get you down," Renée said. "We simply need to find out who the last magical person was to wear that ring."

"Or wait for the coroner's report," I said.

"My way sounds like more fun." She turned in the opposite direction of Sunny Meadows. "Now tell me more about Esme's ghost healing you."

"Where are we going?"

"To talk to Deb about who found the ring," she said. "From what I overheard in the parking lot, she's going out to the trail to pick up the finger you saw."

"Is part of being Grand Witch knowing everything about everyone?" I teased.

She blushed. "I'm still getting used to the title."

"What do you mean? Is it a recent thing?"

"Only since Esme died," she said. "She was the Grand Witch before me."

My heart sped. "Esme was the Grand Witch?"

"And a much more deserving witch than I."

I was having trouble processing all of this. I could feel my hair changing from the follicles to the ends of each strand. It was like sensation overload.

"I'm sorry," she said. "I thought Bernardo told you."

He hadn't.

A realization came over me. I hadn't checked my text messages since I'd headed out to the caves with Xander. Bernardo had told me he wanted to visit, and then I ghosted him.

I pulled out my phone and, sure enough, there were several texts from Bernardo.

Two days ago:

How about soon? As in a couple of days?

One day ago:

I didn't expect not to hear from you when I told my staff I'd be taking a trip.

I may have also booked a flight.

Today:

If you don't want me to come, tell me now or forever hold your peace.

Boarding my flight.

Just landed. If you don't want to see me, I understand. I'll simply visit my cousin instead.

The last one came in minutes ago. My heart felt like it was physically beating out of my chest.

"Ooh, why the sudden hair change?" Renée said.

I glanced at my hair, which was now a bright bubblegum pink. "Bernardo is coming."

"That'll be nice. You deserve to have a visitor after we solve this case."

"No," I said. "I mean, he's coming *now*. He'll be in town in a couple of hours."

"A couple of hours?" Renée's eyes widened. "Then we need to make quick work of this." She stomped on the gas.

We made it to the park in record time. I didn't know what was going faster—the tires or my heartbeat.

How would I handle having Bernardo here? After everything with Xander? I'd kissed them both within the last month. I had feelings for both.

"Stop thinking about it," Renée said. "Warlock troubles always work themselves out. Right now, we need to figure out who had on that ring last."

We got out of the car and started toward the trail, but Deb was already walking back to the parking lot.

"You didn't need to come out here," Deb said. "I found the finger. I'm surprised it wasn't hidden in a better place."

"It was underneath a bush," I said. "If I hadn't been lying on the ground, I probably wouldn't have seen it at all. And we're not here because of the finger. I wanted to ask you who turned in that ring?"

"Melly May's ring?" Deb asked.

"Yes," I said.

"Please, spare no details," Renée said.

"I don't know that I should discuss this with *both* of you."

"I'm a friend of Lucy's," Renée said. "I promised I'd

help her find out what happened to Melly May."

"Just what we need, another amateur sleuth." Deb rubbed the back of her neck with the hand that wasn't holding the clear plastic bag with a detached finger.

"Trust me. I don't have the time to be a sleuth. This is simply a favor for an old friend."

"Good to know," Deb said, her tone sarcastic. "Fine. There's not much to tell. One of the park volunteers—Trisha Bremmer—brought it to us after a hiker gave it to her."

"So a hiker found it?" I asked.

"A couple of them," Deb said. "Trisha told me the hiker found it just sitting on a rock."

"After all this time? It was just sitting on a rock?" I considered this. "Did she say who the hiker was?"

Deb's face lit up in recognition. "I didn't think to ask. Honestly, I didn't know it was anything special until Misty saw it and ran to the bathroom to throw up."

"Did Misty touch the ring?" I asked. "Or put it on?"

Deb shook her head. "She wouldn't get anywhere near the thing. I don't think she wants any more evidence suggesting her sister isn't alive somewhere."

"Back to the hikers," Renée said. "We need to figure out who they were."

"To do so, we'll need to talk to Trisha." Deb pulled out her notebook and flipped through a couple of pages. "I have her number here."

"Do you want to call her, or do you want me to?" I asked.

"Who's the police officer?" Deb said, but her voice was joking. "I'll call her."

I watched as the seconds ticked by. If Trisha didn't get here quickly, I wouldn't be able to talk to her.

"Are you late for something?" Deb asked.

"Someone," Renée said.

Deb smiled. "Xander? I hear he and Laura split."

Renée glanced at me out of the corner of her eye.

"Not Xander," I said slowly. "His name is Bernardo. He's Xander's cousin."

"The one you met in Argentina?" Deb said. "Bex told me about him."

"He's dreamy," Renée said. "If only I were younger."

Deb shook her head. "If he's related to Xander, I'm sure he is."

"He's like Xander with an extra dose of spice." Renée brought her fingers to her mouth and imitated a chef's kiss.

"He's definitely spicy," I said.

"He's coming from Argentina to visit you," Deb said. "Why don't you sound more excited."

"I am," I said. "And nervous."

"Because you're torn between two men," Renée said.

"Don't be the rebound," Deb said. "If I've learned anything, people need time to heal after a breakup. Have fun with Bernardo and wait until Xander is ready. From what I heard, he was pretty torn up when Laura dumped him."

"Why did she dump him?" Renée asked. "I thought they were doing okay."

"So did Xander," Deb said. "But Bex told me Laura was tired of hearing so much about Ellie. Apparently, that's all Xander talks about. He wouldn't even tell Laura about his family or where he lives."

"He's secretive like that," I said with a smile.

"But if he talked about Ellie all the time, would it really be a rebound?" Renée put her hands on her hips and shrugged.

I glanced at my watch and looked for an approaching vehicle.

"Maybe," Deb said. "But I guarantee Bex would tell you to wait if she were here. Xander might have a deep-rooted thing for Ellie, but it sounds like he was pretty taken with Laura."

"How can anyone be taken with Laura?" Renée said, sticking out her tongue.

"Renée!" I stared at her open-mouthed.

"What?" Renée glanced down at her nails. "It's true. She's boring. And not terribly pretty."

Deb snickered.

"Stop," I said. "Both of you. Laura is a sweet girl."

"No. She's not," Deb said.

"She has good qualities," I said.

"Name one," Renée said.

"She can decorate a bench really nicely." It was all I could come up with on the spot. Certainly, there was more, but it didn't matter. Renée and Deb both doubled over in laughter.

"I'm sure that's exactly what a guy is looking for in a woman," Deb said between gasps and laughs.

"Hello," Renée said, impersonating a man. "Do you know how to decorate a bench? Good, we should get married."

They both laughed harder.

I chuckled. I couldn't help it. Their laughter was contagious.

"Seriously," I said, trying not to smile. "Stop. Maybe that's not why Xander dated her, but it is one of her good qualities."

"Or maybe she's just good in bed," Renée said.

Deb stopped laughing. My smile drooped.

"Or maybe not," Renée said. "Goodness sakes. By the look on your faces, you'd think I'd just run over your dog."

The thought of Xander sleeping with Laura wasn't nearly as bad as someone running over Penelope, but it wasn't something I wanted to spend any time thinking about either. Thankfully, I wouldn't have to. A car pulled into the parking lot and stopped right next to Deb's police car.

When the woman got out, I recognized her from another case. She wore a volunteer t-shirt that stretched tight over her pregnant belly. At that moment, I knew exactly who had given her the ring—Orson and Jerri. He'd mentioned something about the pregnant volunteer.

"Thanks for coming," Deb said. "I didn't realize you were pregnant. We probably could have discussed this over the phone."

"It's okay," Trisha said. "My boyfriend's with the little one. It's good for me to get out. Plus, I wanted to make sure I showed you exactly where I found the ring. Sometimes, this park can be tricky to navigate."

"You're telling me," I said.

She turned and looked at me, one hand on her stomach. "It's nice to see you again."

"You too," I said. "How are things?"

"Everything is normal like I like it." She was hinting at me not divulging the reason I knew her. She had once had an affair with a movie star. Jake and I promised not to tell anyone, but if that baby came out looking like it belonged in Hollywood, she'd have a lot of explaining to do.

Either way, it was not my problem.

"Let's walk and talk," Deb said. "Ellie has somewhere to be."

I felt terrible making the pregnant lady wobble all the way back to where she found the ring, but I didn't want Bernardo to show up at my house without me being there. Who knew what Penelope would do to a strange warlock?

"What did the person look like who brought you the ring?" Deb asked as we started down the trail.

"It was a man and a woman," Trisha said, confirming what I'd suspected. "It was really early in the morning. They were holding hands, but the woman was definitely more excited to be here than the man."

"Did they seem prepared for a hike?" I asked.

She shook her head. "But most people aren't when they come out there. People don't think of Iowa as the place to go hiking. Then they get here and realized they're completely out of their depth."

"Do you remember what vehicle they were driving?" Deb asked. "Or anything else about them?"

"I never saw them in the parking lot," Trisha said. "The only other thing I remember is her telling me they were just stretching their legs a bit."

It was them. Orson and Jerri had found the ring. But had they actually found it, or had they had it all along?

We curved around the same path Xander and I had taken, past the cliff. Then, in a direction I'd never been before. My thoughts were racing.

Had Orson and Jerri killed Melly May? Maybe Jerri was going to come clean, so he killed her too. The missing fingers from both bodies and the fact that Melly May had presumably died falling over Deadman's Falls since that's where they found her finger. And then Jerri had died from falling over a cliff.

"Are you thinking what I'm thinking?" Renée whispered as we followed behind the other two.

I nodded. "We need to find Orson soon."

Deb glanced over her shoulder at us and shook her head.

We both nodded our silent agreement not to say anything about the connection in front of Trisha.

"It's right around this corner," Trisha said.

When we turned past a huge rock, an old abandoned

house came into view.

Chills filled my body. The urge to vomit from the coroner's office returned.

"They said they found it here." Trisha pointed to a rock next to the boarded-up door of the house. "Just sitting on top of that rock."

Of course, the house wasn't made of marshmallows as it had been in my dream, but it was made of rounded stones that looked a bit like them.

"Do people normally come back here?" I asked, my throat dry.

Both Deb and Renée glanced at me with worried looks on their faces. Apparently, my voice had given away my fear. Or maybe it was my hair.

"All the time," Trisha said. "It's one of the prime spots for visitors in the summer. People think this place is haunted. We've even had ghost whisperers, and television shows film up here."

"Since when?" I asked. Esme had only died last year.

"Since the park opened," Trisha said. "This was one of the earliest settlements. Even before Iowa became an official state."

"It was a single woman, right?" Deb asked.

Trisha nodded, her eyes lighting up. "The stories about her are epic."

I glanced down at my phone. I wanted to hear the stories, but I didn't have time. "I have to go," I said. "But is the park open after dark?"

"It's open twenty-four hours," she said. "There would be no way to close it."

"Great," I said. "Maybe I'll come back and look around

a bit more if Bernardo will come along with me. Renée, can you please take me home?"

"I'll stay and see if I can pick up any additional evidence," Deb said.

"I'd love to stay and help," Trisha said.

Deb shrugged. "I'm fine with it. Just don't touch anything until I have a look at it first."

Renée and I walked back up the trail to her car. "You know, your workouts are the only reason I'm able to do this right now," Renée said as we got to the top of the hill. "Before I started working with you, I was practically crippled."

"It's too bad we can't use our powers to heal ourselves."

"It keeps us honest," she said. "And mortal. Can you imagine being able to keep yourself alive forever?"

I considered it. Living forever didn't sound like something I'd want to do. But allowing myself to die when I knew I had the power to prevent it would probably be nearly impossible.

"That abandoned house—the one the settler woman built," I said, and Renée nodded. "It was in my dream. That's where Esme healed me."

"I'm not surprised by that at all," Renée said. "That settler woman they were talking about back there was your great great—a few more greats—grandmother. She was the original Grand Witch of the States."

I stopped in my tracks just before Renée's car.

"I've had two Grand Witches in my family?"

"Darling," she said gently, "every woman in your direct

line besides you and Emily have been Grand Witches. I'm only a fill-in until you can take my place."

That did it.

The entire contents of my breakfast came up on the grass.

"I guess I'm glad we didn't have this conversation in my car," Renée said.

I heaved again.

"I probably shouldn't have told you like that. I'm sorry."

She held my hair back as I wiped my mouth with the back of my hand, then wiped it on my pants.

I stood, the nausea subsiding. "What if I can't do it?"

"Only time will tell," Renée said. "Are you going to throw up again, or do you think we can get you home and cleaned up before Prince Bernardo shows up?"

"I'm okay," I lied. I mean, I wasn't going to throw up, but I was the furthest thing from okay. There were so many thoughts buzzing through my head, I could hardly focus on any of them.

We drove in silence—Renée allowing me time with my thoughts. Not that I could think about much of anything other than how ridiculous it was for me to become the Grand Witch.

Me.

The girl who couldn't even use her magic properly.

The girl whose magic was entirely out of control.

I laughed.

"Laughter is better than throwing up," Renée said. "Sometimes, it helps to talk things through. Thoughts can seem enormous in our heads, but when they're voiced, they're usually more manageable."

I highly doubted these thoughts would be more manageable if spoken aloud. It wasn't every day you found out you were destined to be a Grand Witch.

"Don't you think it's a bit ridiculous that they would even consider me as a choice for the next Grand Witch?" I blurted out.

"Not at all," Renée said. "It's in your blood."

"But my blood left me—abandoned me," I said. "And why doesn't Emily have to take on the role?"

"Emily is missing." Renée didn't add the other possibility, even though I knew we were both thinking it.

"What if I find her?"

"It's possible the reason she's missing is that she didn't want to become the Grand Witch at all."

"Then I'll find her and convince her," I said.

"Or you could just accept that you're the next Grand Witch."

"What if I don't?"

Renée slammed on the brakes, the car skidding on the gravel.

She turned and looked at me, keeping her hands tight on the steering wheel. "I will not always be as young as I am right now. As I said, I am only temporarily the Grand Witch. If, when the time comes, you decide not to become the Grand Witch, all the Devil's land will break loose."

She wasn't kidding. Whether she was exaggerating or not, I didn't know.

"What do you mean?" I asked. "What will happen if I don't accept my role as Grand Witch?"

"I'm not authorized to tell you." She pushed on the gas, and we went flying down the gravel road faster than before.

"You're the Grand Witch," I said. "How can you not be authorized to tell me?"

"I have bosses too. And they'd be downright furious with me if I went above their heads."

"Then I want to talk to them."

"No."

"No?"

"No."

"No? Just like that?"

"I said no, and I meant it. No. N. O. No."

"Because you won't let me or because they don't want to speak to me?"

"Both."

I crossed my arms over my chest and slumped back. "I'm not going to become the leader of magic. It's not going to happen."

"We'll see about that."

26

We didn't talk the rest of the way to my house. When the car stopped in my driveway, I got out. "I can get myself together."

"And we can talk to Lucy once we have more information." Renée didn't even put the car in park.

"Have a good night."

"You too," Renée said.

I closed the door of her car and instantly regretted leaving the conversation on such an icy tone.

I turned as she started to back out and waved my arms in the air.

She didn't see me at first as she was looking over her shoulder.

I ran after her car. But, before I could stop, she turned, saw me, and slammed on the brakes.

I smashed into the hood of her car, flat as a pancake.

She put the car in park and flung her door open.

"You do know it's easier to off yourself if you stand behind a vehicle that's backing up."

I groaned. "I wasn't trying to off myself. I was trying to get your attention."

She closed her door and walked to the front of the car. "Do you need help getting off my hood? Should I get a spatula?"

"Very funny." I stood. "I didn't want to let you leave after I was so mean."

"You weren't mean," Renée said. "You were honest. You can always be honest with me."

She opened her arms, and I fell into them, tears seeping out of my eyes.

"Now, now," she said. "This won't do. You have a gorgeous, spicy man coming at any moment. We can figure out the rest of your life later. Enjoy tonight."

She pulled back and wiped the tears from my face.

"Esme would have been so proud of you," she said. "And she would have wanted you to be happy. We just have to figure out what will make you happiest."

I didn't want to talk about being Grand Witch again. We didn't have time to start that argument all over. "Thanks, Renée."

"You're welcome, my dear. Now go get all gussied up."

There had been no need for me to hurry home. I'd taken a quick shower, put on my cutest pair of jeans and a nice blouse, done my hair, and even applied some makeup. But here I was, three hours later, sitting in the window waiting for a man.

Gah. I was so stupid. I should have been out solving the case. He could have texted me when he got here.

I searched online for his flight into the nearest international airport. It had landed hours ago.

Penelope nuzzled me for the thousandth time.

"It's okay," I said. "Though I think you would have liked Bernardo."

She oinked and nudged my phone.

"I already checked. He hasn't texted."

She oinked again, more loudly.

"What is it?"

She wiggled her nose on my phone screen and somehow got into the texting app where Bernardo's last text sat staring up at me.

Unanswered.

"Shoot! I never replied," I said as I typed out a response. "He's probably halfway back to Argentina by now."

I'm so sorry I never replied. I'm still getting used to having a cell phone. Long story. I hope you're still around. I'm excited to see you.

I pushed send and waited.

When I didn't get a reply within ten minutes, I stopped staring at my phone.

Penelope oinked and ran out the piggy door. I followed. Maybe she'd heard something, and Bernardo was here. But when I got outside, she was simply relieving herself.

"Gah!" I yelled. "I'm such an idiot."

Penelope looked at me with wide eyes. I stormed out of the house and into the barn. I needed some time with the mural, even if it was still all black and creepy.

Maybe it would give me some perspective as to what to do with my life now that I'd messed everything up with not one but two gorgeous, amazing guys and basically held a middle finger up to the Grand Witch and all things magic.

I pulled back the curtain, my frustration coming out in the amount of force I used, causing the curtain to unclip from the rod I'd hung it on. It fell on top of me as I crumpled to the ground.

"This is the worst day ever."

Penelope's footsteps made circles around the curtain as if she was trying to get me out.

I crawled toward the back of the barn, half-heartedly pushing the heavy fabric out of my way. It had taken hours to put up the curtain, and I'd taken it down in one hard yank.

It was kind of how Renée's words felt when she told me I would be the Grand Witch one day.

"Grand Witch. Ha!" I laughed. "If only the big bosses could see me right now. They'd realize how unreasonable it was to want me to be their next Grand Witch. I can't even use my magic to get out from underneath a silly curtain."

I finally hit the edge of the fabric, only to find two gorgeous faces smiling down at me.

27

"I take it Renée gave you the big news," Xander said.

He and Bernardo wore matching smiles as they each reached for one of my hands to help me up.

"I don't know why one of you couldn't have told me," I said.

"We can talk about that later," Bernardo said, his English tinged with an Argentinian accent. "Right now, I need a hug."

I didn't have to look at Xander to know he was watching as I wrapped my arms around Bernardo's neck, and he lifted me off the ground.

"I missed you," he said, pulling back and leaning down to kiss me.

I turned my head to the side, his lips coming into contact with my cheek.

My gaze fell on Xander, whose face flashed something I hadn't seen before.

Jealousy maybe?

He turned away and used his magic to put the curtain back up.

"I—uh—missed you too," I said, pulling away and smiling. "I'm really glad you didn't go back to Argentina when I failed to text you."

"Xander and I were having a drink at the bar near his apartment," Bernardo said.

"But we're here now," Xander said, cutting him off. "Maybe we should all get some dinner."

"Dinner sounds great," I said.

Penelope oinked at my feet, and I realized I hadn't introduced her to Bernardo.

"I'm so sorry," I said, lifting her into my arms. "Bernardo, this is Penelope—my best friend in the entire world."

Bernardo grabbed one of Penelope's feet and bent down and kissed it like he was kissing the back of her hand. "It is a pleasure to finally meet you, Miss Penelope. I have heard so much about you."

Penelope oinked, and I could have sworn her pink cheeks got pinker.

I giggled. "I think she likes you."

"She likes everyone," Xander said.

"Except you," Bernardo said. "Especially when you make a pass at Ellie."

"You told him that?" Xander asked me.

"We talked about many things," Bernardo said, scratching Penelope behind one of her ears.

I thought back to the time we spent together in Argentina. It seemed a lifetime and a world away. But the memories made me smile. "It was a fun trip."

"You will have to come back and visit again," Bernardo said. "This time, we will not make you think there has been a murder."

Xander laughed. "With Ellie around, you never know—there might actually end up being a murder."

I pushed his arm. "Hey!"

"It's true," Xander said with a teasing smile. "She's working a case as we speak."

"Is that so?" Bernardo asked, but my gaze had shifted away from the two men to the mural on the back wall. Tingles in my scalp told me my hair was changing before Penelope warned me with her oink.

"How long has it been like that?" Xander asked.

"This is the first I've seen it," I said.

"Is this your mother's mural?" Bernardo asked. "It is beautiful."

It was beautiful but confusing. The dark tunnel with a pin-prick of light was gone, replaced with a painting of an old-timey diner and a gorgeous pink sunset in the background.

"Have you ever seen this place before?" Xander asked.

I shook my head. "Not that I can remember. I've been a lot of places, but I feel like this would have been one where I would have visited, taken a photograph, and eaten dinner. Or breakfast."

I took a step toward the mural. Silhouettes of people crowded the inside of the diner, but only one person stood out front—a woman with white hair and a waitress apron tied in a bow behind her back.

"Do you think that's me?" I asked.

"You're a waitress," Xander said, then quickly added,

"among other things. It only makes sense that it would be you."

"But that's not Katie's," I said. As I examined every stroke of a paintbrush that hadn't actually touched this wall, I searched for the edges of the magic. The sparkles. Anything I could touch that might give me a bit of insight into what it was telling me.

"I do not mean to break up the party," Bernardo said. "But I am starving. And I would like to hear about your case on the way to dinner."

I tore my gaze from the mural and turned to the two men, who seemed to have been exchanging a meaningful look but stopped when I saw them. "What was that?"

"What was what?" Xander asked.

"That look you two just shared." I put my hands on my hips. If they were plotting something again, I didn't want to be the odd one out.

They both acted like they had no idea what I was talking about.

I took one last glance at the mural and turned back to them. "All right, let's go."

I put Penelope in the house and told her not to wait up before grabbing my satchel.

Xander had his truck. Bernardo helped me into the middle of the front seat. Right between the two men who held pieces of my heart.

I told them about the case on the way there, leaving out the pieces about the coroner's office with Neve since I'd promised.

We arrived at an Italian restaurant not too far down the road, and my mouth instantly watered. The food here was delicious. Bonnie—one of the newest Cliff Haven residents—owned it. I'd been on one date here with Bonnie's son—or at least I'd thought it was a date. He'd informed me halfway through that it was merely a business dinner.

He'd died later that night.

Not that I killed him.

Tricking me into a fake date wasn't enough for me to kill someone.

"Table for three?" the hostess asked when we walked in.

Xander nodded, and she led us to a circular table where, once again, I sat between the two men.

"Now," I said. "How about the two of you tell me about this Grand Witch business?"

"There's not much we can tell you," Xander said.

"What exactly does the Grand Witch do?" I asked. "I feel like if I'm going to consider taking the job, I should know what the responsibilities are."

"You can't be seriously considering not taking the job," Xander said.

"Why can't I?" I asked.

"Because the magical world needs you," Bernardo said. "Without a Vanderwick as the Grand Witch, things will go loco."

"Renée isn't a Vanderwick," I countered.

"Renée isn't a permanent Grand Witch," Xander said. "The council approved a temporary appointment until you could be located and trained."

"The council?" I asked. "What council?"

Xander and Bernardo exchanged another look.

"You two are infuriating," I said. "Just tell me. I have the right to know, don't I?"

Bernardo spoke first. "The council is the ruling body over the entire magical community throughout the world."

"They're the Grand Witch's boss," I said.

Bernardo nodded.

"Then I would like to speak to the council and ask them why they think I need to be the one who becomes Grand Witch instead of Emily," I said.

"You can't just speak to the council," Xander said. "There are hurdles you have to go through first."

Bernardo raised an eyebrow at Xander, but Xander ignored him.

"I love hurdles," I said. "I could have gone to state for hurdles when I was in high school. Bring on the hurdles."

"Slow down," Xander said. "We can deal with the hurdles when the time is right."

I sat back in my seat and crossed my arms over my chest. "If his council wants me to become the Grand Witch, the least they can do is talk with me about it."

"If they don't think you're willing to become the Grand Witch, they won't want to waste time talking about it," Xander said.

"Maybe they should have spent their time looking for Emily to get her to become the Grand Witch," I said.

"They did," Bernardo said. "Especially when they did not know you existed."

"They just stopped when they realized I was a possibility?" I asked. "Or is Emily dead, and no one wants to tell me? Is everyone worried I won't be able to become Grand Witch or something if I know Emily is dead?"

They both shook their head.

"That's not it at all," Xander said. "Emily stated multiple times that she never wanted to become the Grand Witch. Even if we find her—"

"When," I corrected.

Xander nodded. "When we find her, she likely will not want to be the Grand Witch."

"So, she just gets off the hook while I'm over here completely unable to use my powers, and this council you talk about wants me to be the head of the magical community in the United States. What kind of requirements does it take to be on this council because they sound like a bunch of idiots?"

Bernardo glanced at Xander, a smirk on his face.

"You really shouldn't speak of the council like that," Xander whispered.

"Well, maybe if I do, they'll come talk to me."

"Oh, someone is coming to talk to you," Bernardo said, looking over Xander's shoulder. "But it is not a council member."

Xander and I turned in unison to see Bex and Laura marching over to our table.

"Do you mind if we join you?" Laura asked, sitting next to Xander without us agreeing.

Bex pulled a chair between Xander and me and gave me a huge hug. "I've missed you so much."

"Same here," I said, hugging her back. There was so much I wanted to tell her, but I was pretty certain I wasn't supposed to discuss matters like potentially becoming the Grand Witch with a non-magical person.

"And who is this?" she asked when we separated. She was positively glowing—her dark skin dewy, her eyes sparkling. Vacation looked good on her.

"I am Bernardo," he said, taking her hand and kissing it. "You must be Bex. Ellie told me all about you."

"Good things, I hope?" Bex said with a slight giggle.

"Absolutely," he said.

I glanced over to see Xander and Laura in what looked like a deep conversation. I couldn't see Xander's face, but

Laura looked like she had been crying. She was also severely sunburned.

"Did you come here to find us?" I whispered to Bex.

"Laura was drunk when she texted him," Bex said. "Then he didn't reply to any of her other text messages afterward."

The thought of my kiss with Xander popped into my head. I felt like a bowling ball had settled in the pit of my stomach.

"Can I bring some additional drinks?" the waitress asked.

"I'll take a water," Bex said.

"And I'd love a blended margarita," Laura said. "Extra tequila."

"Looks like your trip helped her blossom," I said to Bex, just now noticing the low-cut top and tight skirt. Not to mention the alcohol-heavy margarita she'd just ordered.

"She needed to do some blossoming," Bex said. "I just hope she doesn't wilt anytime soon."

Bernardo casually rested an arm across my shoulders. If it had just been the three of us, I wouldn't have allowed it, but since it appeared Xander was getting back with his ex-girlfriend at present, I wasn't too terribly worried about how he felt regarding Bernardo's physical affection.

Bex gave me a sly grin. "Deb told me you have a new case."

"We thought it was Melly May," I said. "Then I thought it was my mom, and now I'm not entirely sure, but it seems like it could be Melly May."

"Really?" Bex asked. "That's sad. I bet Misty is beside herself."

Her mention of Misty reminded me I needed to talk to her about the case. "She seems to be taking it hard. She barely identified the ring and was wasted the last time I saw her. But we do think we know who the murderer is— he likes to cut off women's fingers before he pushes them over cliffs or waterfalls."

"That's disgusting."

"Yeah," I said. "Xander and I talked to him a couple of times before we knew he had anything to do with it."

"How scary," Bex said.

"You're telling me." I leaned back into Bernardo a bit, and he kissed the top of my head. "I just hope they find him. He could be pretty much anywhere by now."

"Don't tell me to hold on," Laura's voice rose above the noise of the restaurant.

When I glanced over, Xander's gaze was directly on me, and his eyes were wide.

For a minute, I thought it was because of Bernardo's and my PDA, but he raised his eyebrows and pointed across the room.

Right where he was pointing was the man I had just been talking about. Orson was at a booth all by himself.

Watching us.

I didn't know what to do.

I needed to call the police, but he would probably run if I did. And I'd end up running after him.

Which was dangerous.

But I couldn't let him get away.

"What's the deal?" Bex asked, noticing the change in my expression and possibly my hair.

"Don't look now," I said. "But the man who killed those women is sitting in a booth across the restaurant."

"The guy staring at us?" Bernardo whispered in my ear.

I nodded slowly.

Laura was still shouting at Xander, but he didn't seem to notice.

Xander turned back and looked at the man, who rose to his feet.

I did the same, anticipating a chase. "Call the police."

Bex pulled out her phone.

Xander and Bernardo were both on their feet as well.

Laura had finally stopped screaming and was looking around, confused.

Orson seemed frozen in place.

"Yes, the man who killed those women is here," Bex said behind me as she spoke with the dispatcher on the phone.

"I don't want to hurt anyone," Orson said, pulling a gun from behind his back, pointing it to the ceiling, and firing off a shot.

Chaos ensued.

Screams echoed through the dining room.

Some people hid beneath their tables while others ran for the doors.

Plates and glasses clattered to the floor as a server dropped a full tray and darted back into the kitchen.

"You don't want to do this, Orson," Xander said. "Just turn yourself in, and everything will be okay."

"Everything won't be okay," Orson said. "I killed her. I did it, and they know I did. I'll rot in jail."

"Why did you do it?" Bernardo asked.

"Who are you?" Orson asked.

"My name is Bernardo," he said. "I am Xander's cousin."

Orson waved the gun around as if he didn't really need the answer.

"Can you tell us why you did it?" Xander asked.

"I don't have to explain anything to you," Orson said. "Or anyone else."

"She knew too much, didn't she?" I asked.

"Knew too much about what?" Orson said.

"The ring," I said. "And how you got it."

Orson waved the gun around in my direction. "She found that stupid ring, not me. And if we would have simply gone back to the car when we found that pregnant trail lady, we wouldn't have been trapped in the wilderness until after dark."

"Why did you cut off their fingers?" I asked.

"Their fingers?" He laughed. "You think I killed both of them?" His eyes widened. "Is that what the police think, too? That I'm a serial killer?"

"Are you?" Bernardo asked, utterly unfazed by the gun being waved in our direction.

"There is no serial killer," Orson said. "I cut off her finger to make it look like it was a serial killer. One of the other hikers was talking about the woman whose finger was found a few years back. If only my car hadn't been stolen, I would have gotten away with it."

Lights flashed through the windows. The police were here.

"I can't go to jail. I wasn't made for jail. Or hikes. She knew that. She did it on purpose. She deserved to die." He fired the gun at the ceiling again and then ran toward the kitchen.

A fresh wave of screams echoed from behind the swinging doors. Then a gunshot rang out.

Xander had an arm around Laura's shoulder as she hugged his middle and cried.

Bernardo and Bex stood next to me as we recounted what happened to Deb.

"He said he didn't kill Melly May?" Deb asked.

I shrugged. "He could have been lying."

"We'll find out eventually," Deb said. "As soon as we get the coroner's report back."

When she'd come inside, she informed us that Orson had tried to use the shoot into the air scare tactic with the police. It hadn't worked. One of the officers tackled him—a move that was currently getting the officer a stern talking-to by one of the other officers—and Orson had been taken into custody. He wasn't talking and had requested his lawyer.

"Should we go back to my place?" I asked. "I'm sure I can whip up something to eat."

Our waitress emerged from the back and handed us two huge bags. "Your food, plus some extras."

"I guess I won't have to cook after all," I said.

"Thank goodness for that," Bex said with a laugh. "I mean, you do a good job with popcorn and peanut butter, but that's about it."

Everyone else laughed too.

"Penelope doesn't mind my cooking," I said. "And it's much better now that I have access to a whole kitchen."

"I would have hated to try it when you cooked out of your van then," Xander said.

Even though he was teasing just like Bex had, it still stung. But I laughed along with everyone. Early in life, I'd learned that if I laughed along with people, they didn't tease me nearly as much.

"I'm sure Ellie's food was fantastic," Bernardo said, interlacing his fingers with mine.

I smiled at him. "Thank you."

"Why don't the two of you ride with me," Bex said to Bernardo and me. "We'll let those two have the ride to themselves so they can figure things out."

When I glanced up at Xander and Laura, Xander's attention was on my hand in Bernardo's. But when Laura spoke, it quickly shifted to her.

"I think that's a great idea," Laura said.

Xander nodded in agreement.

That settled it then. He and Laura would get back together, and I'd get to spend time with Bernardo without feeling guilty about Xander's feelings.

It was nice that someone had made that decision for me, but for a second, I considered whether that's the decision I would have made for myself if given the opportunity.

When we got back to my house, I turned on a movie, and we ate like kings and queens. I made a mental note to tell Bonnie how wonderful her staff had been. Maybe she'd give them raises or something.

The next morning, as the sun streamed in through the windows, I glanced around at my living room. Bernardo was fast asleep in a chair. Laura and Xander were tangled up in each other's arms on one of the sofas.

Jealousy hit me like a freight train. I'd done my best to ignore them all night. I'd even done my fair share of cuddling with Bernardo. But the sight of them asleep together, looking so serene, made me want to puke.

I quietly stood from the couch, so I didn't wake Bex and Penelope—who looked rather cozy together—and tip-toed outside. The air was chilly this early in the morning. Spring was beautiful in Iowa, with all the grass turning green and the trees budding, but the weather was unpre-dictable. Some days were warm, and others felt like winter was still trying to edge its way back.

The barn, however, was perfectly warm.

I fired up the coffee pot and waited for it to finish brewing before taking my mug of energy bean juice to the back, where the mural still held the painting of the diner.

I sank into the oversized plush couch and took in every bit of the mural between sips. The colors were vibrant in the sky—a pale turquoise now—and the woman stood with her back to me and her apron on just like before.

"Who are you?" I asked aloud. "Are you me? Or are you Emily or Esme?"

The painting didn't respond. Not that I expected it to.

"I wish I could talk to someone about this Grand Witch business. Someone who would actually give me some answers." I sighed and took another sip.

"I guess you're in luck," a voice said behind me.

I turned to find Lucy standing in my barn. It was the first time I'd seen her in regular clothes instead of the pretty house dresses she always wore when I visited her at Sunny Meadows.

"What are you doing here?" I asked.

"I needed to talk to you without anyone else around." She sat in one of the chairs close to the couch. "Renée is great and all, but she is very guarded with her information."

"Everyone seems to be." I stood. "Do you want a cup of coffee?"

"That would be lovely. With cream and sugar, please."

I poured her a mug. "Are you really going to tell me whatever I want to know?"

"As long as I know the answers," she said. "But I want something from you in return."

I handed her the coffee and sat back on the couch. "What would that be?"

"I want you to find the truth about Melly May."

"You don't think Orson killed her like he killed his wife?"

She took a sip and smiled. "This is excellent coffee. And no." Her smile disappeared. "I don't."

"Me neither. But I'm not sure what else I can do."

"Start with Misty," Lucy said. "I don't believe anyone has ever asked her about Melly May's disappearance."

"You think Misty killed her twin?"

"Oh no. Not at all. But Misty was with Melly May the day she died."

"Are you sure?" I thought back to Esme's notes. They specifically stated Misty had an alibi.

"I raised those girls," Lucy said. "They were always together."

"But if they were together, the police would have had to talk to Misty."

"Misty took the entire thing really hard. She never was one to take things very well, but losing her sister—her best friend in the entire world—was one of the biggest blows she'd ever been dealt. I was worried for quite some time that we'd end up losing her too."

"Do you think it's possible Melly May died by suicide?" I asked.

"Not a chance," Lucy said. "She was terrified of heights. If she had killed herself, it wouldn't have been by throwing herself over the falls."

"Maybe she didn't throw herself over the falls," I said. "If she's who I found in the cave, maybe the finger had been dropped near the falls to make people think she'd jumped."

"That's entirely possible."

"That would mean someone killed her."

Lucy shrugged. "It seems like the only option, doesn't it?"

"I'll do my best to talk to Misty about it," I said. "Now, I want to know who makes up the council."

Lucy laughed. "You don't hold back, do you?"

"I need to speak with them."

"Knowing who is on the council is one thing," Lucy said. "Speaking to them is entirely different."

"Why?"

"They only get together once a year. And they typically book out years in advance."

Frustration crept up my neck. "Then can you tell me who they are?" I considered trying to track each and every one of them down.

"The council is made up of witches and warlocks who have taken an oath to serve the magical community by whatever means necessary."

"Names," I said. "I want names. I need to find them and tell them I don't want to be the Grand Witch."

"And whyever not?" Lucy said, her tone shocked.

"Because I can't even control my hair," I said. "How am I supposed to be the queen of all the witches in my country?"

"Esme couldn't control her hair either, and she was a brilliant Grand Witch, just like all the Grand Witches before her."

"What does the Grand Witch do?"

"She keeps the database of all witches in the states and their abilities. When there's a breach of magical law, she can track and find whoever it was so they can be punished. She makes suggestions to the council about improving the worldwide magical community. But she also does various charity work, hosts events and people in her home, and will occasionally cure people—magical and not."

Everything she talked about lined up exactly with the abilities I had.

"The Vanderwicks are the only magical family with both the ability to track and the ability to heal," Lucy said, confirming my thoughts.

"And what happens if I choose not to become the Grand Witch?"

"Then it'll go to someone else. Or, rather, two someones."

"Two?"

"A witch and a warlock," Lucy said. "One with the ability to track and the other with the ability to heal."

"And is there something wrong with these two? Is that why everyone is so adamant about me taking the title?"

"Some people question their motives for stepping forward," Lucy said. "They don't exactly have the cleanest backgrounds."

"Couldn't they find different people?"

"If they wanted to rewrite the job description, I suppose they could." She thought about this for a moment. "But I don't know what the purpose would be of a Grand Witch who couldn't heal or track. It would just be a witch with a crown."

"There's a crown?" I laughed. The idea somehow struck me funny. "I was only laughing about the queen thing."

Lucy raised her eyebrows, then laughed too. "Of course, there's not a crown. I was just joking."

"I've asked everyone else this, but I'll ask you as well."

"Go ahead," Lucy said.

"Why isn't my mother next in line for Grand Witch?"

"For the same reason, you can't find her," Lucy said. "She doesn't want to be."

30

Her admission was like a gut punch.

It was something I already suspected but didn't want to know for certain. Now that I did, part of me felt hopeless.

I glanced up at the mural where the woman slowly faded until she disappeared entirely.

I gasped. I'd never seen it change before my eyes.

"That's a fine piece of magic you have right there," Lucy said, standing. "I'd keep it protected."

"I'll talk to Misty today and let you know what I find out," I said, not taking my eyes off the mural.

"You don't need to tell me," Lucy said. "When you figure it out, tell the police."

I must have sat there for an hour after I heard the door close behind Lucy. The diner painting was still there, but the colors were less vibrant, and the woman hadn't reappeared.

When the door cracked back open, I turned to find

Bernardo with a sleepy look on his face and his hair a curly mess.

"I wondered where you had slipped off to," Bernardo said, his voice deep.

"I needed coffee and to think about some things."

"Like that kiss you shared with Xander?" He didn't look at me as he poured himself a cup of coffee.

"I'm surprised he told you."

"I'm not," Bernardo said. "We have always been very close."

He sat next to me on the couch.

"I feel you and I have a connection, but I sense you and Xander may have a connection as well."

I couldn't get any words out, so I just nodded.

"I can imagine it is hard for you to see him with Laura."

I nodded again.

He reached out and took my hand. "What can I do to help?"

"I need to take my mind off of it," I said.

Before I could get any other words out, Bernardo leaned over and kissed me, sending fire through my veins.

"That's not exactly what I was thinking," I said when he pulled back. "But it was nice."

He took my coffee out of my hand and put both our mugs on the table in front of us. I closed my eyes as his hands cupped my cheeks and his lips pushed up against mine again.

What started sweet quickly turned steamy like it had in Argentina. With my eyes closed, it was almost like we were back there, dancing the Tango. The smell of the spicy food and the sound of the accordion filled my ears.

His hands didn't stay on my face but found their way to my lower back and then to my own hands. He pulled me to a stand, and we were kissing and dancing. I stood on my tip-toes so my stilettos wouldn't get stuck in the cobblestones that clicked under our feet.

A woman sang along with the accordion and piano in a language I didn't understand. But I didn't have to understand it to know she was singing about love. Passion.

Mid-kiss and mid-step, I felt a firm hand on my shoulder.

I opened my eyes to find myself back in my barn. On the couch. Barefoot and in pajamas.

The music was gone. Bernardo sat in front of me, his hands still cupping my cheeks, with a smile on his face.

The hand on my shoulder squeezed tighter.

When I glanced to my right, Xander stood staring down at us.

"Where'd you take her?" Xander asked his cousin.

"Where else? Argentina." Bernardo dropped his hands.

"You—we were—how?" I asked.

Bernardo grinned, making my insides twist with desire. "Magic."

"That's enough magic for now," Xander said. "Jake's here, and he wants to talk to you."

Xander turned and walked out of the barn without so much as a glance back.

Bernardo leaned forward and gave me one last kiss. "Thanks for going with me."

"I—uh—you're welcome?"

He pulled me to a stand and handed me my coffee mug.

I turned the coffee pot off as he and I walked out of the barn hand-in-hand.

Jake sat at the dining room table with his mug of coffee. Bex must have made some in the kitchen.

"Hi, Jake." I sat down, and Bernardo sat next to me.

Jake eyed Bernardo.

"Oh, this is Bernardo. I met him in Argentina. He's Xander's cousin." Nothing I said seemed to change Jake's expression.

"It is a pleasure to meet you," Bernardo said.

Jake ignored him and turned to me. "We found blood in the car, and it came back as Melly May's."

"She's alive?" I asked.

"That's one possibility," Jake said.

"And the other is?" Bernardo asked.

Jake turned to him and glared.

"It could actually be Misty's," I said. "Since they're identical twins?"

Jake stared at Bernardo for one last second, then looked at me. "Exactly."

"You think Misty stole Orson's car from the park?" I took a sip of my coffee.

"She came in drunk with that nasty gash on her head," Jake said. "It makes sense."

"But why?"

"I think finding the ring sent her back over the edge."

Jake sipped his coffee. "We worked really hard with her when she started at the station, but I think she's fallen back into her old ways."

"What old ways?" I asked.

"Drinking, drugs, erratic behavior." Jake shook his head. "She never was as stable as Melly May."

"It sounds like you are saying you wish she had died instead of her sister," Bernardo said.

Jake ignored him, but Bernardo had a point.

"I need to talk to Misty," I said. "Do you know where she is?"

"Probably at home," Jake said. "I'll come with you."

"Do you mind if I speak with her alone first?" I asked, remembering my promise to Lucy. She'd never said I couldn't have Jake there when I spoke with her granddaughter, but I suspected she'd frown upon it. "It might embarrass her to talk about things with you since you're her boss and all."

"Sure," Jake said. "But we better get going. The Des Moines news just got hold of the case. I suspect we'll have news crews lining up in front of the police station to get information within the hour."

"I will stay here and clean up." Bernardo leaned over and kissed me on the cheek. "Be careful."

I blushed at the PDA in front of Jake. "I will. And thanks."

"Anything for you," Bernardo said.

When Jake and I were inside his police car, he said, "I thought you had a thing for Xander."

"Bernardo and I had a great time in Argentina," I said.

"I guess I never thought he'd end up at my house. But I have to admit, I like him."

"He rubs me the wrong way," Jake said.

"Because he's foreign?"

"Because he's a man who has an obvious interest in my non-daughter." Jake winked. "I've never been a faux-father before."

My chest warmed, and I could see my hair turning pink from the corner of my eye. "It's okay."

31

I don't know what I expected Misty's house to be like, but I hadn't expected a beautiful, brand-new construction on the south side of town.

"It doesn't look like anyone's home," I said.

"Her car is probably in the garage," Jake said. "She hasn't been at work since the drunk incident. Deb came by last night and talked to her for a while, but she said Misty was drunk then too."

"I'll let you know when to come in," I said. "I shouldn't be long." First, I needed to figure out what the heck was going on and why Lucy wanted me to talk to her so badly.

"Take notes about anything she says."

I rang her doorbell no less than three times and knocked more than that, but there wasn't an answer.

The curtains were pulled tightly closed, so there would be no way to see inside.

Jake rolled down his window.

"I'll try the back door," I said.

"She has a dog," Jake said. "I'm surprised it's not barking at us."

"What kind of dog?" Hadn't Lucy said a dog attacked Misty, and she now feared animals? Or was that Melly May?

"A big one. Be careful."

Maybe she'd gotten over her fear. Pets were practically the best things ever. Before I'd gotten Penelope, I'd tried to rescue a dog but never found one that seemed right for me. Probably because I was meant to find Penelope.

"Hello? Doggie?" I called over the fence, making sure a pair of teeth wouldn't come into contact with my leg the moment I opened the gate.

The backyard was empty, and when I got to the sliding glass door in the back, it was partially opened.

I glanced around again but didn't see anyone.

I slid the door open the rest of the way and walked inside, instantly regretting my choice.

Within seconds, my feet were back outside, and I was at Jake's window. "I think she's dead."

Jake clicked his mic and called for backup. "Stay here." He rushed through the back gate and out of sight.

I tried to process what I'd seen. Blood. Lots of blood. And Misty lying on the tile kitchen floor.

Dizziness washed over me. I sunk to the ground and let my head fall into my hands.

A strange sensation came over me. It was as if I'd dipped the backs of my hands into warm water.

I uncovered my face to find massive teeth and a tongue dripping with drool in front of me. My body froze. Would it bite me?

Then it lowered itself into my lap and whimpered.

The brown and black furball must have been Misty's dog. I stroked its fur and felt extreme sadness wash over me.

I retracted my hand, and the sad feeling subsided.

Occasionally, I could sense feelings from people, but I'd never experienced it when it came to animals. At least, not that I was aware of.

I stroked the dog's fur again, and the feeling came back. When I looked closer, the dog had specks of blood on its coat. I needed to tell Jake about it, but I couldn't pull myself away from the sad pup. It had seen its owner die. Just the thought of Penelope having to watch me die was enough to bring tears to my eyes.

A siren coming up the street brought me back to the situation at hand.

An ambulance pulled into the driveway, and two paramedics quickly got out.

"Go through the fence into the back of the house," I said, though I wasn't sure why they were there. Probably just to pronounce her dead.

My mind went to Lucy, and my heart dropped. Now, she'd lost two granddaughters.

The paramedics came rushing back out with what looked like a body on the stretcher.

I scrambled to my feet, the dog following suit, to see what they were doing. Had there been someone else inside?

Jake hurried out behind them. "I just hope we found her in time."

"What do you mean?" I asked, getting a glimpse of

Misty's face between the paramedic's arms. The dog rushed to their sides and tried to jump up to see her.

"She was still breathing," Jake said. "She's lost a lot of blood, but she might make it."

I glanced at the paramedics, who weren't loading her into the ambulance.

"Why aren't they leaving?" I asked.

"They're waiting on a life flight," Jake said. "If she's going to have a chance at survival, she needs to get to a big hospital as quickly as possible."

Without thinking about it a second longer, I rushed to Misty's side and pressed my hands on her wounds. I closed my eyes and concentrated, sending my healing magic into her body.

When I opened my eyes, I expected to see her eyes open and her wounds healed. Like in the movies. But she looked the same. Maybe slightly less pale, but more or less the same.

I hadn't noticed the helicopter had landed in the middle of the street until a piece of my now-black hair blew across my face and got stuck between my lips.

I held tight to Misty's dog, covering his ears and letting him bury his head in my legs as they loaded Misty into the belly of the helicopter and took off.

As if he knew, the dog started barking at it, asking it to bring her back.

"It's okay," I said. "They'll take care of her."

The dog hushed and looked at me for further comfort.

I bent down and hugged him around his neck. "Do you want to come home with me while she's gone?"

"You don't have to do that," Jake said. "He can come with me."

"I don't mind," I said. "But before we take him anywhere, we need to clean him up. He has blood all over him."

Jake paused. "What do you mean, he has blood all over him?"

I showed him where there were blood spots near the dog's mouth and down its front.

"We need to take samples of this," he said. "Maybe the dog bit whoever attacked Misty."

If only I could communicate with animals, maybe the dog could tell me who did it.

An idea popped into my head.

My magic might not have been talking to animals, but someone's might. I only needed to speak with the Grand Witch so she could access her database.

Jake took samples from the dog while I called Renée.

"Have you seen Lucy?" Renée said without even saying hello.

"I did this morning," I said. "She came to visit me in my barn."

"That doesn't surprise me. Did she tell you where she was going?"

Now that I thought about it, she hadn't. "I assumed she was going back to Sunny Meadows."

"Well, she didn't," Renée said. "She wasn't supposed to leave in the first place."

"It's not like it's a prison," I said. "Isn't she free to come and go as she wishes?"

"Yes, but she's not allowed to drive."

"Maybe she didn't," I said. "Maybe she hitched a ride."

Renée thought about this for a minute, then said, "Thanks. Gotta go."

She disconnected before I could get my question out.

I dialed her number again. It rang twice. Then there was silence on the other end.

"Hello?" I asked.

"Is this Evelyn?" Renée asked.

I laughed. "No, it's Ellie."

Renée paused, probably looking at her phone.

"Who is Evelyn?"

"No one," she said. "How did I call you?"

"You didn't. I called you back."

"Why? You already helped me."

"Right, but I needed to ask you a question," I said. "That's why I called before."

"Oh." Renée seemed very confused. "Go ahead then."

"Do you know anyone who can speak to animals?"

"Why?" Renée's voice turned suspicious.

"I found a dog I need to get some answers from," I said. I didn't want to tell her about Misty yet, mainly because I didn't want her dropping the news on Lucy without me being there.

"Is it a magical dog or a non-magical dog?" Renée asked.

"There's a difference?" My mind felt like it might explode.

"No," Renée said. "I'm just kidding with you."

I did not find her funny. "Is there someone in your database with the ability to speak with animals or not?"

Renée didn't respond for a long time.

"Are you there?" I asked.

"How did you know about the database?" Renée asked.

"Someone told me," I said. I wasn't about to throw Lucy under the bus.

"Well, they shouldn't have. You need to accept becoming a Grand Witch without knowing all the perks."

"Do you know someone?" I asked again. "If you don't, I'll leave you to find Lucy."

Renée sighed. "I do, but they're difficult to get in touch with."

"Are they local?" I asked.

"Not in the slightest," she said. "But they can be here within a day or so if they feel like it."

"Can you compel them?"

"I'd need a pretty solid reason to compel a witch to do my bidding."

"What if it has to do with the safety of another witch?"

"Why didn't you say that in the first place? Who is the other witch?"

"Can I convince you without telling you who?"

"No."

"Fine," I said. "But you can't tell Lucy."

"I knew it. Lucy's in trouble, isn't she?"

"No," I said. "At least, not that I'm aware of. I'm talking about Misty. Someone attacked her this morning in her home, and I think the dog saw who did it."

"I'll get in touch with the witch and ask her to make a trip to Cliff Haven," Renée said. "But in the meantime, can you please help me find Lucy?"

These witches and their trading favors for favors. If I wasn't careful, I'd be indebted to everyone around me. "I'd be happy to."

We disconnected, and Jake came walking out of the police station with a sopping wet pooch. The dog shook, soaking Jake, but Jake didn't look irritated by it at all. In fact, he laughed.

"I miss having a dog," he said. "I haven't had one since I joined the police academy. I didn't feel like it was fair to have a pet when I wasn't home to take care of it. But maybe I'll ask Georgia . . ." His words trailed off, worry overtaking his features.

"How is Georgia?" I asked, keeping my voice upbeat.

He looked relieved that I wasn't upset to be discussing his fiancée. "She's better now."

"What do you mean?"

"She was pretty irritated that we had to come back from our trip," he said. "But she got over it."

"Maybe she'll want a dog as much as you do."

I rubbed the pooch behind his wet, floppy ears. "We should take this guy to my house and leave him with Penelope. She'll keep him in line."

"Are you sure?"

"Definitely." I didn't tell him that there was a possibility of a witch communicating with the dog. Not that he would have freaked out, it just wasn't a for sure thing, and it wouldn't be admissible in court, anyway. Kind of like the feelings I got every once in a while.

Jake loaded the dog into the back of his patrol car.

"Will he get your back seat dirty?" I asked.

"The back seat might get him dirty," Jake replied with a laugh. "You'd be shocked how many people have thrown up back there. And it's so hard to get vomit out of carpet. Thank goodness for leather seats."

Jake drove us home, dropped us off, and waved goodbye.

"Come on," I said. The dog hadn't been wearing a tag, and Jake couldn't remember his name. "Dog, come."

Thankfully, he responded to Dog.

Penelope charged out of the house, oinking like she was a guard dog. Misty's actual guard dog hid behind my legs.

"It's okay. Penelope is nice." I looked at Penelope. "Be nice to our guest."

She ducked her head and did the pig version of tiptoeing over to Dog. Dog finally came out from behind my legs and sniffed Penelope. Within minutes, they seemed like best friends.

Once inside, I closed the pig door from the inside of the house so Dog couldn't get out. Penelope protested but eventually gave in.

Bernardo wasn't lying when he said he'd clean up. Everyone was gone, and the house was spotless. Maybe he'd used his magic—and if so, I needed in on that trick—but it didn't matter. The house looked amazing.

"You two be good while I'm gone," I said, giving each of them a kiss on the head and heading outside.

I hopped into Mona and headed toward Renée's house. My mind focused on Lucy. "I need to find Lucy."

As if she had a mind of her own, Mona's gas pedal depressed, and we took off. Just like when we'd almost hit Orson.

"Mona," I said as calmly as I could. "We have to pick up Renée before we find Lucy."

But she turned in the opposite direction of Renée's house, down another gravel road.

"Where are we going?" I tried to hold on to the steering wheel, but I was obviously not in control. Not that I felt unsafe. But it was like driving a self-driving car without it actually being a self-driving car.

"If you know where Lucy is, that's great, but we should get Renée first."

My phone rang in my satchel. I picked it up and fumbled to get it to my ear. "Hello?"

"Where are you? I thought you were picking me up?" Renée sounded irritated.

"Trust me. I wish I were," I said. "I think I focused too intently on Lucy's whereabouts while holding onto Mona's wheel because she's decided to take off again."

"Mona? As in your van?"

"Is that strange?" I asked. "Do vehicles usually have magical abilities?"

Renée was silent for a moment, then said, "Some do."

"Well, I think I'm driving one." I laughed. "Or she's driving me."

"Ellie, are you certain you were focused on Lucy's whereabouts when you held onto the steering wheel? Or is it possible you were thinking about something else?"

"I was definitely thinking about Lucy's whereabouts. I figured I'd get a head start on tracking her so we could just be off when we got to your house. But Mona turned us down a gravel road away from your house."

"Do you know where you are?" Renée asked.

I looked around. "Not really. But I can send you my location."

"I'll get in the car right now."

Mona took a right turn at a speed I never would have dared go while driving her. Maybe this was her way of telling me she could handle a bit more speed.

"I hope you're having fun," I said. "Because this is nuts."

She took another turn, this time directly into a cornfield.

"Okay, Mona, you're scaring me." I tried to stomp on the brakes, but she wouldn't stop. I tried to turn the wheel, but it wouldn't turn. "We don't need to find Lucy if it ends up killing us."

I closed my eyes and tried to bring my magic to the forefront. I could overcome this. If I could be the Grand Witch of the States, I could control my microbus.

When I opened my eyes, the cornfield had shifted into a neighborhood of outlandish tiny houses.

Magical tiny houses.

It was a magical place I wouldn't have been able to see without searching for the magic within. I'd only ever seen two others before—the pond behind my house and the car dealership where I'd gotten Mona. From Xander's father.

Mona slowed to a stop in front of an extra-eccentric tiny house. Not only was it five stories tall, but each level of the house was also a different color, offset, and seemed to be tipping. Like building blocks that might fall at any moment. On the front porch were plastic figures of some sort of winged creatures. And the grass was bright pink.

"This is where we needed to go at such a pace?" I asked, grasping Mona's wheel. "We could have died."

The wheel warmed beneath my touch, almost as if she was trying to apologize. "It's okay. You did what I asked you to. Even if I didn't know, I'd been asking." I would have to be more careful next time. It seemed like as my magic grew, so did Mona's.

I stepped out of the car, and the smell of homemade cookies fresh from the oven hit my nose. I closed my eyes and inhaled.

"Are you going to come in and have some or just stand out there forever sniffing the air like a puppy dog?"

I opened my eyes to see Lucy standing in the front doorway of the block house.

"Renée has been looking for you," I said.

"She just wants to put me back into that assisted living community."

I shook my head. "I don't know about that, but I'm pretty sure she wants to tell you about Misty."

"What's wrong with Misty?" Lucy asked.

I glimpsed someone peeking out the window of the house next to Lucy's.

"Someone attacked her this morning. They flew her to the hospital in Iowa City."

"Oh dear," Lucy disappeared into the house and was back outside within seconds, holding a purse. "Can you take me there?"

"Absolutely," I said. "But maybe we should wait for Renée to catch up."

"Do you think we have time for that?" Lucy said, allowing me to help her into Mona's passenger seat.

Just then, I saw Renée's car approaching as if it had appeared out of thin air. All of this magic was starting to freak me out, and I'd lived with color-changing hair my entire life.

Renée jumped out of the car. "We have to get to the hospital."

"Do you want to ride with me?"

"In a van with a mind of its own?" Renée said. "No thanks. I'll drive myself. Just follow me. I know a shortcut."

I hopped into the driver's seat and tore off after Renée.

"What is this place?" I asked, trying to get a view of the town around me while still focusing on the road.

"It's Cliff Hallow," Lucy said. "The magical alternative to Cliff Haven."

"Does every city have a magical alternative?"

"Wouldn't that be grand?" Lucy asked. "But sadly, no."

"But if Cliff Hallow exists, why did Esme live in Cliff Haven? And Renée too?"

"People with magic can live wherever they wish to live," Lucy said, her hands wringing in her lap. "Do you think Misty will be okay?"

"Let's hope so." I pushed more firmly on the gas pedal, and Mona picked up speed. Cliff Hallow vanished in a heavy fog—so thick I almost couldn't see Renée ahead of us. I started to slow, but Mona apparently didn't want me to.

"Mona," I said, a firmness in my tone.

"My car always used to give me fits too," Lucy said. "Wanna know a secret?"

"Any bit of help would be great." I gripped the steering wheel so tightly I thought I might leave indents from my fingers.

"Loosen your grip on the wheel and give her a good tickle right here." Lucy pointed at the flat piece of the dash just below the radio.

"Tickle her?" I asked without taking my eyes off the fog. I was certain at any moment we'd go smashing into the back of Renée's car, killing us all.

"And tell her exactly what you need her to do." Lucy looked at me expectantly.

I reached a finger out before the rational side of my brain took over and tickled the dash. "Mona, I want you to do as I ask, even if that goes against what you think is right."

"That's good," Lucy said. "But you might not be so hard on the old girl. She's much wiser than you give her credit for."

I tickled again. "Please, slow down just a bit. At least until we get out of the fog. Then we can do as you see fit."

As if by—well, magic—Mona slowed.

When the fog parted minutes later, we were on the interstate, almost at the exit for the hospital. Mona was still in control, and Renée was only a couple of car lengths ahead of us.

"How did we get here so quickly?"

Lucy looked at me as if I was dumber than a bikini in a snowstorm.

"Right, magic."

We rushed into the emergency room waiting area to be told we'd have to wait. Magic could get us to the hospital quickly, but it didn't necessarily make the doctors perform their surgery more quickly.

Only a few minutes after we sat in the less-than-comfy chairs the nurse at the desk had pointed out for us, Jake came barreling through the doors.

He looked at me with confusion all over his face. "How did you—"

I stood to meet him.

"Never mind. I don't want to know." He ran a hand over his hair. "It probably involves speeding. How's the dog?"

"Hopefully, fine," I said, then turned to Lucy. "Do you know what Misty's dog's name is?"

"Misty has a dog?" Lucy asked.

"A big one," I said. "Apparently, she got over her fear.

I've just been calling him Dog, but knowing his name might make things easier."

Lucy wasn't listening. She was staring off into space.

"Lucy," I said. "Are you okay?"

"I just can't believe she has a dog," Lucy said.

I felt terrible for Lucy. It had to be hard to be separated from your own granddaughter—to know nothing about her. I almost turned back to Jake, but something caught my eye. The frayed hem of Lucy's jeans looked like it had been dyed red. Or soaked in blood.

I weighed my options. Tell Jake or ask Lucy first? Maybe she had a perfect explanation for it. Maybe it was beet juice or her own blood.

"A dog?" Lucy mumbled, still not looking at us.

Jake touched my arm and lowered his voice. "Are you okay?"

"Look at the bottom of Lucy's pants," I whispered. "I think that might be blood."

"Are you implying she may have had something to do with . . ." Jake's voice trailed off as we watched Lucy.

"Do you want a cookie?" Lucy asked, pulling a massive Ziplock bag of chocolate chip cookies from her purse.

"When did you make these?" Renée asked, taking one.

"This morning," Lucy said.

"Why?" Renée asked, examining the cookie.

Lucy shifted in her seat again, setting the cookies down next to her. "Because I was craving chocolate chip cookies."

"We've been friends long enough for me to know the only time you crave chocolate chip cookies—and then make said cookies—is when you've done something bad." Renée gave Lucy a serious look.

Lucy's eyes widened, then filled with tears. "I should have called the police right away, but I didn't want to go back to the assisted living center, and then you were there, and—"

"The police?" Renée interrupted, then glanced over at Jake.

"What did you need to tell the police?" I asked Lucy.

"I was there," Lucy said, tears now dropping down her cheeks. "I saw it happen. After talking to you this morning, Ellie, I decided I would put all the old stuff behind me and go see Misty. But when I got there, someone else was already inside. She and Misty were fighting about something, but I couldn't hear what. The door was locked, so I went through the back. When the other woman saw me, she ran, but she'd already wounded Misty. I tried to stop the bleeding, but there was so much blood. Then I heard you knocking on the front door, so I ran out the back. I knew if you saw me there—especially since Misty and I didn't always see eye to eye—you'd think I did it."

"Back up," I said gently. "Do you know the woman who attacked Misty?"

Lucy shook her head. "I couldn't see her face. She was wearing a black hood over her head. But she was very fat. Or maybe pregnant."

Pregnant. Like Trisha.

"Did Misty ever have a friend named Trisha?" Jake asked his mind on the same track as mine.

"No," Lucy said. "But Melly May did."

"I think we need to talk to Trisha," I said. "She is the one who turned in the ring, after all."

Lucy stood. "Trisha turned in the ring? Melly May's ring?"

"A hiker brought it to her, and she turned it in to the police," I said.

"And you believed her story?" Lucy seemed utterly shocked.

"Why wouldn't we?" Jake asked. "Is there something we need to know about her?"

"She may have been Melly May's friend, but they always had a healthy rivalry," Lucy said. "Maybe she's had the ring all this time."

"I questioned her myself when Melly May went missing and again when we found the finger," Jake said. "She had a solid alibi."

"Doesn't mean she didn't do it." Lucy sat back down. "And if it was her today with Misty too?" Lucy shuddered.

"If Misty wakes up, I want to talk to her," Jake said. "I'll ask one of the nurses to call me when that happens. Then we can head out to talk to Trisha."

I nodded, and he walked away, leaving Renée, Lucy, and me staring awkwardly at one another.

"Are you certain Trisha was the one attacking Misty?" I asked Lucy. "Because you said she was fat but other than that, you couldn't really identify her."

Lucy shrugged. "If it wasn't her, then I guess I'm wrong. But it makes plenty of sense to me. She killed one twin and then went after the other."

Several years later and while she was with child. That didn't seem realistic.

"I tried to heal her," I said, my voice quiet.

Renée and Lucy both glanced up at me.

"Misty," I said. "I tried to heal her before they took her away in the helicopter. But I failed. She was still bleeding and unconscious."

Renée and Lucy exchanged a knowing look.

"I wish everyone would stop doing that," I said.

"Stop doing what?" Jake asked.

"Looking at each other like they had secrets—secrets from me, *about* me." I stood.

Jake, Renée, and Lucy stayed silent.

"Ugh, whatever," I said. "Let's go."

"Before you go," Renée said, standing and looking at me. "Can I have a quick word with you?"

"Sure," I said.

Jake nodded. "I'll meet you outside."

"Are you going to explain that look to me?" I asked.

"If Misty survives this, it may be due in large part to your magic," Renée said. "Just because you didn't see its effects doesn't mean it wasn't working."

"And that's what the look was about?" Embarrassment flooded my cheeks and sent my scalp tingling. I'd over-reacted.

"Yes," Renée said. "Now, you need to know that the magic we did moving quickly between Cliff Hollow and the hospital—you can't do that with Jake. I know Mona will do whatever you ask her to, but there are boundaries on how we use our magic around the non-magical."

"Should I not have healed Misty with non-magical people around?" I asked. Maybe that was why they exchanged the look.

"We can talk about the rules in more detail later," Renée said. "What you did in trying to save Misty was well-intentioned and on an emergency basis."

That sounded like code for I wasn't going to get in trouble, but I could have.

"I won't use Mona's magical driving with Jake around," I said. "And I'll be careful about my magic around the non-magical."

This seemed to appease her. We said our goodbyes, and I hopped into Mona's driver's seat. I tickled the dash and said, "I'll drive this one."

She started without a hitch and let me take the controls.

"Thanks, Mona."

Her steering wheel warmed in my hands.

We followed Jake back to Cliff Haven. It was excruciatingly slow. If Renée hadn't warned me, I probably would have tried to use it and then ended up in hot water with this council of witches and warlocks who remained nameless but had all the authority over everything.

Ugh.

When we pulled into Cliff Haven, I felt like I'd been in the car for hours. It was almost like driving cross-country when you were used to flying.

Jake knocked on Trisha's door, and we waited.

A child cried in the background, and when Trisha opened the door, she was wearing a black hoodie.

"I suppose you're here to take me to jail," Trisha said. "Hey, babe?"

A man appeared behind her. "Yeah?"

"Can you watch the baby? I'm being arrested."

"That was quick," he said, picking a toddler up off the floor behind her. "Just call me when you need to be bailed out."

She turned around and put her hands behind her back so Jake could cuff her.

"I don't think I need to cuff you," Jake said.

She turned back around and shrugged.

He read her the Miranda rights, then said, "Would you like to tell us what happened?"

"She killed her sister just like I always knew she had."

"And you know this, how?" Jake asked.

"I saw her put the ring on the rock for those people to find," Trisha said.

"Why didn't you come to us about this?" Jake asked.

"I did. I told you Misty was responsible. She was always jealous of Melly May. And why wouldn't she be? Melly May was perfect. Absolutely perfect. She would have done so much more with her life than Misty has." She glanced at Jake's badge—the same one Misty wore. "No offense."

"None taken," Jake said.

"But why would Misty want someone to find the ring?" I asked. "If she killed her sister, don't you think she would have wanted the ring to stay hidden?"

"Who knows," Trisha said. "She probably just wanted more attention. After the finger was found, she got a ton of media attention."

"So you let the hiker find it and give it to you, you turned it into the police, and then you confronted Misty," Jake said.

"I went to her house several times, but she was never home, until today. I just wanted to talk to her, but she kept trying to explain herself. I didn't need to hear excuses or reasons why she killed my best friend." Trisha rubbed her belly. "We were supposed to leave this town together. Get married together. Have kids together. And Misty ruined all that. She thought I'd be her friend after Melly May died, but there was no way I wanted to hang out with that loser."

"So you tried to kill her?" I asked.

"Tried?" Trisha said.

"She didn't die," Jake said. "We found her in time."

I thought I heard Trisha cuss under her breath.

"All right," Jake said. "Let's get you down to the station."

When she was all loaded up in the back of his police car, he turned to me.

"Do you think it's possible Misty killed Melly May?" I asked.

"I think anything's possible," Jake said. "But Misty loved Melly May. They were practically best friends. And Melly May was the only person who seemed to love Misty at times. It was slightly heartbreaking."

"Then why would she have had that ring?"

"I think we need to ask her that when she wakes up."

My phone pinged in my satchel—a text from Renée.

Misty's awake.

"Looks like we can do that now," I said.

"That was fast," Jake said. "I'll take Trisha down to the station and let them book her, and then I'll meet you at the hospital. If she says anything of importance before I get there—"

"I know," I said. "I'll write it down."

Jake looked at me with pride. "You sure you don't want to join the police force?"

"Pretty sure," I said. "But thanks."

He got in his car and sped off.

I thought for a minute. Since Jake wasn't following me, I could technically do the super-speedy driving thing, right?

I slid into the driver's seat and closed my eyes. "Mona, I want to do the speedy magical thing, but I don't want to crash and die, and I don't want any non-magical folks to see."

I opened my eyes to find fog surrounding us.

Mona's engine cranked easily. I tickled the dash and said, "Fast but careful, please."

She took off, and in the blink of an eye, we were at the hospital.

"You used the magic, didn't you?" Renée asked when I walked into the emergency waiting room.

"Jake wasn't with me or anything, and the fog came, so I don't think anyone—"

"I wasn't asking because I was mad. I was asking because I was impressed. That's some pretty high-level magic."

"It was all Mona," I said. "She took total control."

Renée shook her head. "Mona doesn't have magic without you. She can only do what you empower her to do."

I wanted to disagree. Mona had most definitely done things without my empowerment. But arguing didn't seem like the right thing to do right now.

"Do you want to chat with Misty?" Renée asked. "Or do you need to wait for Jake?"

"He just told me to take notes," I said. "Plus, if she's awake right now, she might not be by the time he gets here."

Renée led me upstairs to a room that looked like they

could have sectioned it off for two people but currently only held one bed.

Misty lay in a mess of bruises and stitches under the white sheets. Her face was almost unrecognizable. She and Lucy seemed to be having a rather intimate conversation, so Renée and I waited in the doorway for them to be finished.

"Can't you heal her?" I whispered to Renée.

"She doesn't want to have anything to do with magic," Renée said. "Since her sister died, she has completely turned away. I would never heal someone who doesn't want to be healed."

"Maybe she'd accept it just this once," I said.

"No," Misty's voice rose. "No magic. Not now. Not ever."

I plastered a smile on my face. "How are you feeling?"

"Like I got attacked by a psychopath with a big knife." Misty pushed the button for the bed to raise.

"Trisha is being booked into jail as we speak," I said.

"Then I suppose it's only a matter of time before I have to tell my story," Misty said.

"What story?" Lucy asked, her voice gentle.

Misty ignored her grandmother.

"If you're talking about the ring, then that would be helpful," I said. "Especially because it doesn't look great for you if Trisha is telling the truth."

"She's telling the truth," Misty said. "I found the ring but was too afraid to turn it in. I knew how it would look. So I left it on that rock and waited for that woman to pick it up."

"At any point, did you wear the ring? Or did you see the woman put it on?" I asked.

She shook her head slowly. "No. Why?"

"No reason," I said. "So they took the ring to Trisha."

Misty grunted. "I wish I'd have thought about the fact that Trisha volunteers at the park. I usually plan my trips on the days she's not out there."

"Do you go to the park often?" I asked.

"Every chance I get," she said. "My sister was my best friend. I like to think she's still out there, listening, and guiding me."

"Like she guided you to the ring?" Lucy asked.

"Not magically, if that's what you're asking," Misty snapped. "But yes."

"Why do you think Melly May would have wanted you to have the ring now?" I asked. "Instead of closer to when she died or in a few years from now?"

Misty's eyes filled with tears. She shook her head and rolled over. "I don't want to talk about it."

Lucy put a tentative hand on Misty's shoulder, but Misty brushed it off.

"Please, just leave," Misty said, her voice cracking with emotion. "I'll talk to Jake when he gets here. But right now, I need my peace."

Lucy, Renée, and I went down to the cafeteria to wait for Jake to arrive.

"I think she did it," Lucy said. "That was all an act. Even though Melly May got all the lead roles in the play, Misty was the one who wanted to be an actor."

"After all these years, you're still too hard on that poor girl," Renée said. "I'll get coffee. Does anyone else want some?"

"Yes, please," I said.

"Not for me," Lucy said, reaching into her purse. "I'm perfectly content with my chocolate chip cookies."

She offered me a cookie, but I wasn't in the mood for food. This case was getting more and more convoluted as time went on.

"I wasn't that hard on her," Lucy said. "I want to see Renée try raising twin girls all by herself."

"What happened to their parents?" I asked.

"They both died in a car accident. It was horrible on the girls," Lucy said. "But especially on Melly May. That might have been why I was harder on Misty because I knew she could handle it."

"How old were they when it happened?" I asked.

"Five," Lucy said.

I'd argue that no five-year-old was tough enough to handle losing both of their parents.

Renée held out a coffee for me and sat at the table. "I know Esme got feelings about cases," Renée said. "Did you have any when you spoke with Misty?"

"Not really," I said. "Though I wasn't thinking about it that much."

"One thing about magic—you have to be aware. It's kind of like when you were living in your van. You had to make sure you were staying in safe places. You watched the people around you." Renée took a sip of her coffee and winced. "It's the same way with your magic. If you want to hone your craft, you have to be constantly aware of the magic within you and the magic around you."

"I'll try to do better," I said. "But that doesn't mean I want to be the Grand Witch."

Lucy started choking on one of her cookies. Renée slapped her on the back. "Cough it up. Come on."

Finally, Lucy regained her breathing. "You're serious about not becoming the Grand Witch?"

"Why does everyone find it so hard to believe I wouldn't want to be the Grand Witch?"

"I don't," Jake's voice came from behind me. "Your mother didn't want to be the Grand Witch either."

"My point exactly," I said. "And she grew up with magic in her life."

"She talked to you about becoming Grand Witch?" Renée asked Jake.

"She talked to me about everything," Jake said. "But I don't think it's strange that she didn't want to. Esme—regardless of how wonderful she was—put a lot of pressure on Emily to hone her magic so she could take over the title someday. But Emily never blossomed under pressure. She wasn't like Esme. She was much gentler and free-spirited. And I see a lot of that in you, Ellie."

I smiled.

"But I also see a strength in you that Emily didn't have," he continued. "An ability to push through when things got tough. If Emily would have had that, she'd probably still be here right now."

"So you think I should become Grand Witch?" I asked.

"I think you should do whatever you want to do," he said. "But from the conversations Emily and I had, it sounds like this Grand Witch business is not only a massive responsibility but also an honor. Part of your family's legacy."

His words hit a nerve in my soul. My family's legacy was to become Grand Witch. Emily might have run from that, but I wasn't a runner. Not anymore. I'd made that determination the minute I'd settled into Cliff Haven.

"How about I think about it?" I finally said.

This seemed to appease Renée and Lucy.

"Did you end up talking to Misty?" Jake asked.

"She said she'd talk to you," I said. "But she was pretty upset when we left."

"Why?" Jake asked.

I gave him the rundown of what we'd talked about.

And then he and I went back up to her room. I planned on staying outside, but Jake insisted I come in.

"Sorry about earlier," Misty said. "I wasn't upset with you. I just can't believe Lucy has the nerve to walk in here and act like she cares about me after all these years."

"Why don't you tell us more about that," Jake said. "Why don't you think Lucy cares about you?"

"Maybe because she favored Melly May every single day since our parents died. No matter how much I tried, she couldn't stop coddling Melly May. Then when Melly May died, she never called me. Not once. I even sent Ellie over there to help with her range of motion, but still, no call."

That didn't sound like Lucy at all. She might have favored Melly May, but she seemed genuinely worried about Misty's well-being. Even if she did think Misty was the one who killed Melly May.

"She came to me this morning and asked if I'd check on you," I said. "She may not show it well, but she does care for you."

Misty didn't reply.

"Will you tell me a bit more about the ring?" Jake asked. "Where did you find it?"

"At the falls," Misty said, her eyes glazing over as she picked at a stray string poking out of the hem of her bedsheet.

"Where?" Jake asked. "The top or the bottom."

"The top," Misty said. "I went up there to talk to my sister. Things were getting so overwhelming, and I thought maybe I could just make them all go away." She stopped and broke down into sobs.

When I reached for her hand, an overwhelming feeling washed over me. But it was more than sadness. I pressed into my magic, trying to be aware like Renée had said.

What was the feeling?

It wasn't anger or fear.

Guilt.

The answer popped into my head as clear as a cool mountain lake.

She felt guilty for her sister's death.

"I know you've been over this before," I said as gently as I could. "But can you tell me about when Melly May died?"

"Why? Because you think I killed her? That I was jealous, so I pushed her over the falls?" She wasn't speaking in an angry tone. More like a matter-of-fact way. "Honestly, I might as well have."

"What do you mean?" Jake leaned in.

"It's my fault she's dead," Misty said. "I should probably just confess and get it over with."

Jake and I exchanged a look. Was she actually confessing to her sister's murder, or did she just feel guilty for something that may have led Melly May to take her own life?

"What do you need to confess?" Jake asked.

"I pushed her," Misty said. "My magic pushed her off that cliff. I didn't mean for it to happen. We got into an argument about how different everyone treated us. She asked if I wanted her just to jump off the cliff. I told her yes."

Jake and I sat watching the poor girl in front of us recount a story she'd kept inside all this time.

"And then she jumped or fell or was pushed by my magic. But the look on her face, before the waterfall engulfed her, was sheer terror. I knew at that moment she hadn't wanted to jump." Tears dripped from her chin and soaked into her hospital gown.

"How can you be certain it was your magic that pushed her?" I asked.

"Because I was horrible and selfish, and my mere existence caused her so much pain."

"But we found her in a cave," I said. "Maybe she didn't die from the fall."

Jake cleared his throat. "I forgot to tell you, the coroner came back and said it's likely the fall is what killed her."

"See? I did it." Misty said. "I should have never become a police officer. I'm so sorry, Jake."

"But you didn't physically put your hands on her, right?" I asked. Jake couldn't possibly arrest her for something she thought maybe her magic did.

"It doesn't matter," Renée said from behind me. "If she used her magic to kill her sister, she has to be punished."

Jake stood and let Renée take over the situation. As Renée told Misty about her magical legal rights, Lucy sobbed.

Something about this wasn't sitting well with me. Somehow, I knew Misty didn't kill her sister. Maybe she was covering for someone. Or perhaps she was afraid of someone. It just didn't add up.

"Do you think she did it?" I asked Lucy while Jake and Renée worked out the details to have a guard posted outside Misty's hospital door at all hours of the day and night until she was healthy enough to be taken to a magical jail.

"I thought she did it from the very beginning," Lucy said. "Of course, my magic doesn't have the sensing power that yours does, but I'd like to think it goes beyond magical ability. No matter how sweet and accommodating Melly May was, Misty was so hard on her. I'm sure she didn't mean to hurt her sister, but all those pent-up feelings had to come out somehow."

I looked over to where Misty seemed in a trance. She held something between her fingers—a charm like the one my mother wore in that photograph.

"May I see your necklace?" I asked.

Misty's gaze focused on me. "Why?"

"Because I think my mother had one like it."

"Everyone who graduates Cliff Haven High has one," Misty said, holding the charm tightly in her fist. Between the look on her face and her defensive posture, I could tell she didn't want me to touch her necklace. It was probably an anxiety-relieving mechanism for her.

"It's okay," I said. "I don't need to see it."

She relaxed a bit as I stepped back toward the door. "When I found Melly May's body, she was wearing hers too. Initially, I thought it was my mother's body. I didn't know every Cliff Haven graduate got one."

Misty just turned her gaze back out the window.

"What happens next?" I asked, walking back to Jake and Renée.

"We'll have a magical coroner examine Melly May's body," Renée said. "If any magic was used in her demise, we'll know."

Misty whipped around to look at us—her necklace still clutched in her hand. "What happened to the ring?"

"I have it," I said, pulling it from my satchel. "Why?"

"I know I'm not allowed to have jewelry in jail, but do you think I could hold on to it while I'm in the hospital?" Misty's eyes were pleading as her face swelled around them.

I glanced at Lucy and Renée, who both shrugged.

Jake said, "I don't see why not."

I handed her the ring, and she slipped it on her finger like that's where it belonged this entire time.

"Thank you," she said, then turned her gaze back out the window.

We started to walk out of her room when I turned back and asked, "One more thing—what's your dog's name?"

"Wix," she said without looking at me.

"As in a candle wick?" I asked.

"With an x—W-I-X." As she said each letter, her voice became more and more full of emotion. "Make sure he finds a good home."

Tears welled in my own eyes. Just the thought of someone else having Penelope made it difficult to breathe. "I'll take good care of him for you."

I followed the other three out of the room into the hallway.

I cleared my throat to regain my composure before asking Lucy, "What's the significance of the ring?" I felt ridiculous that I hadn't asked before now.

"Someone gave it to Melly May her senior year of high school," Lucy said. "A boy, I think."

Jake glanced back at me, his eyebrows raised.

"Do you know the boy's name?" I asked. If there had been a boy, maybe he'd come between Melly May and Misty. Maybe that's the piece I was missing.

Lucy shook her head. "I'd have to think about it. Melly May met him at a magical camp I sent both girls to one summer. Misty ended up having to come home early because of bad behavior. That was one of the worst summers she and I had without Melly May there to act as a buffer."

Lucy may not have known who the mystery man was, but I'd bet Trisha did.

Renée said she'd take Lucy back to Cliff Hallow while Jake and I planned on heading to the station to talk to Trisha.

The drive back was—once again—terribly slow, but I used the time to expand my magical periphery. I searched for magic everywhere. Now and then, I'd see a small roadside business with a funky name that I knew I hadn't seen earlier in the day.

Every bit of magic I saw sent a spark of accomplishment through me. And with every bit I saw, I seemed to see more and more.

When we passed through Poppy Hills—the rival town right next to Cliff Haven—I could see the extra houses in their own little magical village, similar to Cliff Hallow.

Mona chugged along happily, her steering wheel warming and cooling with every new bit of magic I saw. I loved the thought of her magic growing as mine did. Like we were in sync with one another.

When we arrived at the station, Jake went down to the jail to see if it was too late to speak with Trisha. He was the police chief, so he could probably override whatever they said, but it was nice he respected their opinions on the matter.

While he checked, I hung out in the lobby. The receptionist was on the phone, but I was too busy looking for any piece of magic in the police station.

So far, it was completely void.

Until Neve—the coroner—walked in.

A tiny glow surrounded her, and a bit of shimmer trailed after her as she walked.

"Hey Ellie, how you doing?" she asked when she saw me.

"You didn't tell me you were a witch," I whispered so the receptionist wouldn't hear.

Neve's eyes looked like they might pop out of her head. "Why would you think I'm a witch?"

Shoot. Maybe she was like I had been. Maybe she didn't know she was a witch.

"Oh, I'm probably wrong, sorry," I said. "It's been a long day."

"Come over here." She pulled me by my arm to the corner of the room. "You were right, but how did you know?"

"I can see it," I said. "Or sense it, maybe."

"What can you see? Or sense?" Her tone was frantic.

"Just an aura around you—a bit of it trailing behind when you walk."

She let out a curse word, then closed her eyes. "Can you see it now?"

The glow still surrounded her. "Do you want me to say I can't?"

She cursed again. "How?"

But Jake walked back in, interrupting our conversation.

"Don't tell anyone," she said as I walked away.

"What was that about?" Jake asked, giving Neve a strange look over my shoulder.

"She's having some lady problems," I said. "Nothing to worry about."

Jake's face went bright red—the subject officially being closed. "I have Trisha in one of the interview rooms, but let's make it quick. It's almost lights out."

The interview room was a simple concrete room with a two-way mirror on one wall and a metal table in the center. Three metal chairs had been placed so one was on one side of the table—where Trisha sat—and two on the other for Jake and me.

"I already told you everything," Trisha said.

"Did Melly May have a boyfriend?" I asked, sitting across from her. Jake stood back by the two-way mirror.

"Melly May had lots of boyfriends," she said. "You'll have to be more specific."

"One summer, she and Misty went to camp—a camp I'm guessing you weren't allowed to go to."

"The magical one?" She rolled her eyes. "It sounded stupid anyway."

"Misty had to come home early—"

"Because she started a fire and nearly burned the place down."

I filed that away for later. "But on that trip, a boy gave Melly May the ring."

"That's all you had to say. If you'd have just told me about the ring, I would have known who you were talking about. She refused to take that piece of junk off. She died wearing it."

"What was the guy's name?" I asked.

Misty looked at Jake and then back at me. "What's in it for me?"

I heard Jake groan behind me.

"What do you mean?" I asked.

"She wants a deal," Jake said.

"This information might just be the key to the entire case," Trisha said. "Who knows?"

"I thought you said Misty killed Melly May?" I said. "If that's the truth, there is no case."

"If that were the truth, you wouldn't be here asking me about a guy who gave Melly May a ring," she said with a smirk.

"I can't offer you a deal," Jake said. "I'd have to call the District Attorney and—"

"I'm not the one who needs the information," Trisha said, rubbing her pregnant belly. "I can wait as long as I need to."

It was my turn to groan. I looked back at Jake, who shrugged.

"If that's all," Trisha said. "I'd like to go back to my cell. It's bedtime, and I'm quite tired."

Jake led me out of the room and told the officer in the hallway he could take her back down.

"Now what?" I asked.

"Now, we wait," Jake said.

When I got home, I was met with a terrible mess. It looked like every pillow in the entire house had simultaneously blown up, leaving bits of feathers on every single surface.

"Wix? Penelope? Where are you?"

The sound of happy dog feet came bounding down the stairs. When he came around the corner, he had a pillow in his mouth.

"No, no," I said.

He hunkered down with his butt still up in the air, wiggling.

I laughed and lunged for the pillow, but he was too quick. He darted off back up the stairs, ran down the hall, then practically tumbled back down, charged past me, and started doing laps around the main level with the pillow still flopping around in his mouth.

I heard an oink from the top of the stairs and found an exhausted-looking Penelope lying at the top.

"It looks like you had a rough day," I said, walking up to carry her down.

She nuzzled into me and wiggled her nose, her eyes closed.

Wix did another lap, then charged back upstairs, where the footsteps stopped. He was probably making that pillow his next victim. Oh well. He was practically an orphan now. He deserved to have a bit of fun.

I walked outside to let Penelope relieve herself.

"Wix," I called. "Do you need to go outside?"

It sounded like a herd of wild boars charging down my staircase. Wix flew out the door and into the flat field that was actually a magical pond behind the barn.

"He's going to stay with us for a little while," I said. "His mommy got hurt and might have to go to jail."

Irritation flowed through me, and I wasn't sure if it was my own because it didn't seem right that Misty would have to go to jail or Penelope's because she'd have to deal with a four-legged terror for a while. I didn't have the heart to tell her that he'd be living with us forever if Misty went to prison.

"Come on, Wix," I yelled. "Let's get you some food."

He came bounding out of the field, thoroughly soaked.

"How did you get into the pond?" I asked as he flew into the house and shook right in the middle of the kitchen. I'd have to see if there was a magical way to clean a house.

I sucked in a breath and let it out before setting out to make some popcorn with peanut butter—Penelope's favorite.

When the food was done, I followed the muddy paw prints to where Wix stood in the living room, still wet but not on the furniture, so that was a plus.

"Here's your bowl." I put Wix's bowl of popcorn on the floor in front of him. "I'll get you some proper dog food from Fran's Feed tomorrow." He didn't seem to mind as he licked the peanut butter off the popcorn. "And here's yours." I put Penelope's on the couch next to me, where she always sat.

I was about to turn on a movie when the doorbell rang. Wix growled.

"Who could that be at this time of night?"

I let Penelope off the couch, and she and Wix followed me to the front door.

Renée and an ancient witch I'd never met stood on the front porch.

"Hi," I said when I opened the door. "Is everything okay?"

"This is Bathelda," Renée said. "The witch who can speak with animals."

39

Penelope and Wix sat in the middle of the living room with Bathilda.

"It's quite hard to understand them with peanut butter in their mouths," Bathilda said.

"Do they speak to you with their tongues like humans?" I asked.

She looked at me as if I was the dumbest person she'd ever met. "How else would they speak to me?"

Penelope let out a low oink.

"This one is very sensitive to your feelings," Bathilda said. "I won't repeat the words she just said to me."

"Penelope!" I said. "No cursing!"

Renée laughed. "It's not like anyone can understand her."

Bathilda glared at Renée.

"Other than Bathilda, of course," Renée quickly corrected.

"What about Wix?" I asked. "Can he tell you any more about the confrontation between Trisha and Misty?"

Bathilda stared at Wix, their noses almost touching.

Wix let out a groan and laid on the floor at her feet.

"He doesn't want to talk about it," Bathilda said.

I sighed. Dead end after dead end. Not only was Trisha unwilling to talk, now Wix was too?

"Can you compel him?" Renée asked. "This is important."

Was it, though? Trisha already admitted to hurting Misty—attempting to kill her. That was practically an open and shut case.

"I cannot compel an animal to speak any more than I can compel a human to speak." Bathilda turned toward us. "Or are you asking me to torture them to give you answers?"

"No," I said, standing from the couch. "Absolutely not."

Renée laughed. "She was joking, Ellie."

Bathilda, Wix, and Penelope all seemed to be laughing too.

I laughed along with them and sat back down. "How long has Wix been with Misty?"

Wix let out a low growl—not threatening in nature, but more as if he were speaking to Bathilda.

"She got him just after her sister died," Bathilda said. "A young man brought him to her house and left him there."

"Does he know who the young man was?" I asked.

"Just like people, animals don't usually have terribly good memories from when they're young," Bathilda said, not taking her eyes off Wix.

Wix continued to grumble.

"But it sounds like he remembers them kissing," Bathilda said. "And her being sad when he left."

So Misty had dated someone.

"Did he ever go to the state park with Misty? To the caves?" Renée asked.

Bathilda listened for a moment, then said, "He went, but he was too afraid to go in the caves. He preferred to stand guard outside."

"In the caves?" I asked. "How often did she go in the caves?" Misty talked about going to the waterfall, but not the caves. If she'd gone inside, maybe she was the one who took Melly May's body into the crevice. If that was the case, though, why wouldn't she have just told us that? She'd practically confessed that she'd killed her sister. Moving a body wasn't nearly as bad as actually killing someone

"That's all Wix is talking about," Bathilda said. "Is there supposed to be something else?"

"The waterfall," I said. "Did Misty ever take him to the waterfall?"

Bathilda shook her head. "He loves water. He said he would have remembered a waterfall."

"Do you think Wix could take us to the place where Misty would go?" I asked.

"Yes," Bathilda said slowly. "But he doesn't want to go inside the cave."

"That's okay," I said. "He doesn't have to."

I stood and walked to the back door.

"Oh, you want to go now?" Renée asked.

"I won't sleep if we don't," I said. "There's something not sitting right with me."

"You don't think Misty did it?"

I shook my head. "I don't know. But I need to figure it out."

Wix rode with me in Mona's passenger seat while Renée and Bathilda followed behind us.

I picked up my phone and called the police station.

"Cliff Haven PD," the receptionist said.

"Hi, it's Ellie," I said. "Is Neve around?"

"I think she's in the dungeon," she said. "I'll patch you through."

"Thanks," I said with a laugh. I'd never heard the basement called the dungeon.

"Hello?" Neve said.

"Hey, it's Ellie. I have a quick question for you."

"Before you ask," she said. "No one knows I'm a witch. Not a single person. Esme knew, but when she died, the secret died with her. And I'd like to keep it that way."

"That's your call," I said.

She sighed in relief. "Good. Now, what's your question?"

"Renée said there are specific magical coroners," I said. "Ones who can detect whether magic was the reason someone died."

"Magic didn't kill Melly May," Neve said. "Not that I can tell you that officially, but that's what the magical coroner will find."

"So Misty's innocent," I said.

"Unless she pushed her sister over that cliff with her hands."

"Thank you," I said. "Have a good night."

"You too," Neve said. "And thanks for keeping my secret."

"Any time," I said.

We disconnected just as I was pulling into the park. The moon was full, its beams peeking through the tree branches overhead, casting eerie shadows on the ground.

"Let's get your mama home," I said to Wix when I put Mona in park.

ix led us to the exact spot I thought he would—the entrance to the cave where I'd found Melly May's body.

"Do you need to go inside?" Renée asked.

Based on where we were, I didn't need to. But a magical tug inside told me I should.

"You guys stay out here," I said. "I'll only be a couple of minutes."

"What are you looking for?" Bathilda asked. "Wix wants to know."

"I'm not sure," I said. "But whatever it is, the pull is strong."

"Be careful," Renée said as I took the staircase Orson had shown us down into the cave.

Wix barked.

"It's okay. He's just afraid for you," Bathilda said.

"I'll be fine," I said up to him.

My flashlight was bright against the damp cave walls. I

focused on bringing the magic to the forefront. A small sparkle came from the crevice where I'd found Melly May.

As I climbed back there, I felt right where I was supposed to be.

In the tiniest fissure in the rock at the back, the magical sparkle flashed and then went out.

I shined my flashlight where it had been, and the beam reflected off something.

When I reached a hand in, my fingers landed on what felt like metal. I pulled it out to find a necklace just like the one Misty had been wearing in the hospital. Like the one my mother had been wearing in the photograph.

It warmed in my palm as I flipped it over to see the letter M on the back. It was Melly May's.

As I crawled back out of the crevice, the tracking magic that I'd used to find Melly May's body pulsed to life. A new path—the same red color as before—led out of the cave.

My heart quickened. Melly May was the last person to wear this necklace. Maybe it held some of her magic within it and was leading me to where she'd died.

I burst from the cave, running as fast as I could.

Wix barked when he saw me.

"Come on," I said. "We have to follow the trail."

"What trail?" Bathilda asked. "This is torture on an old woman's body."

"Would you like me to give you some relief?" Renée asked as I passed them.

Wix jumped playfully at my excitement, but I needed to keep following the iridescent pathway before me. If it dissipated, I might never know what it led to.

Wix kept a nice pace behind me as I could hear Renée and Bathilda a few yards back. Then a few yards became more as I widened the gap. Renée was the Grand Witch. They'd be okay.

I heard the waterfall before I saw it.

When I came around a turn, the ground opened up into a large pool fed by the churning waters that fell from the cliff above.

The tracing path stopped at the water's edge.

"What am I supposed to find here?" I muttered to myself.

Wix grumbled a bit, but I had no idea what he was trying to tell me without Bathilda there to interpret.

I glanced down to find his gaze fixated on the top of the waterfall.

Someone stood at the top of the cliff, their silhouette black against the huge rising moon.

Wix whimpered.

"Is that . . ?" I squinted, trying to see better. "It can't be."

But it certainly looked like Misty at the top of the cliff.

Wix crouched to the ground and started crawling up the path that seemed to lead to the top of the falls. He glanced back at me, and I didn't need a magical dog interpreter to know that he was asking me to follow him.

I crouched down and followed. If I bolted up there, she might jump.

When we got almost to the top, I could see for sure it was Misty.

Wix stopped, so I did too.

"What are we going to do now?" I asked. I'd never

talked someone off a cliff before. Not literally, anyway.

But before Wix could reply, a voice came from ahead of us. "You don't want to do this."

Another figure appeared in the moonlight.

Lucy.

"You don't know what I want to do," she said. "I'm done keeping these secrets. I can't go to jail. Do you know what they do to cops in jail?"

"You know I love you," Lucy said.

"Do you?" Misty asked. "Are you sure?"

"I sent you all that money when you refused to take my calls or visits."

"You were horrible to me growing up."

"Was I? Are you sure about that?"

Misty didn't reply.

"Because I'm pretty certain I was wonderful to you."

Misty's voice changed. "How did you figure it out?"

"The dog," Lucy said. "Is that why you didn't want me to visit?"

Misty laughed. "Do you think it would have taken a dog for you to figure it out if I was standing right in front of you?"

"Of course not," Lucy said. "I know my granddaughters like I know my own magic. And I know that right now you must be terrified out of your mind to be at the top of this cliff."

"We never could trick you."

The puzzle piece clicked into place, revealing the entire picture.

That wasn't Misty.

It was Melly May.

"Why?" Lucy asked, her voice so quiet I almost couldn't hear it.

"She deserved better," Melly May said. "She deserved to be treated with the same respect I was. I wanted her to have a better life. To be able to leave a legacy."

"But you had such a bright future."

"Not without her, I didn't. She was the other half of me. When she came up here and tried to end it, I lost every bit of spark left within me."

"Tried to end it?" Lucy asked.

"She didn't die from the fall." Melly May's voice cracked with emotion. "I tried to talk her out of it, but she was so tired of living in my stupid shadow. Did you know I was the one who nearly burnt down the camp? But she took the fall because everyone expected it to be her."

"Why would you burn down the camp?" Lucy asked.

"I was a stupid kid—the golden child. And the only reason I was the golden child was because of Misty. She took tests for me when I knew I'd fail. She lied for me when I was out late with boys. She even let that dog bite her so I could get away."

"Why didn't you tell me?" Lucy asked. "Maybe things could have been different."

"I tried, but you didn't believe me. No one did. When Misty died, I couldn't let that be the legacy she left behind. She needed to make something of herself. But I'm no good without her. I'm only mediocre no matter how hard I try."

"I can't lose you again," Lucy said. "Please don't do this."

"You lost me a long time ago," Melly May said, taking a step toward the cliff's edge.

This was it for Wix. He sprang into action, bounding up the path, jumping clear over Lucy's head, and grabbing onto Melly May's sleeve, pulling her back away from the falls.

"Wix? What are you doing here?" Melly May said.

I stood from my crouched position. "He's here to save you, just like Misty would have wanted."

Melly May buried her head in Wix's fur and sobbed.

Lucy rushed to their side and knelt next to them. "I'm so sorry. Please forgive me."

Melly May looked up at her grandmother. I expected her to tell Lucy to leave, but instead, she pulled her grandmother in for a hug.

Wix licked Lucy's face as the two women sobbed.

"Good gracious," Renée said behind me. "Did you have to sprint?"

She and Bathilda looked like they might pass out from exertion.

"I'm glad I did," I said, pointing up at Lucy, Melly May, and Wix.

"Was she going to jump?" Bathilda asked.

"Maybe," I said. "But Wix saved her."

"Good boy, Wix," Bathilda yelled up to him.

He barked back.

We went to the police station at Jake's insistence. When I called him, I thought I could hear some grumbling from Georgia in the background about his work-life balance.

The large conference room was the only place big enough for all of us. Melly May and Lucy sat across the table from Jake, Renée, and me. Wix was curled up at Melly May's feet.

"Can you start from the beginning?" Jake asked. "Tell us what happened."

It seemed like Melly May was all cried out as she started her story. "Misty was planning on ending her life. She left me a note—it's at my house."

Jake waved a hand as if to say she could get it another time.

"It said she was tired of trying so hard and that she was sorry she couldn't be there for me anymore." Melly May sniffled. "I found the note and drove as fast as I could to the waterfall. I tried to tell her to stop, but she jumped anyway."

Wix sat up, and Melly May instinctively wound her fingers in his fur.

"I ran to the pool at the bottom, hoping she was okay," Melly May said. "She was stuck under the water. Somehow, her finger got caught in the rocks. The only way to get her out was to cut it off."

My insides twisted.

"I pulled her from the water and up onto the shore," Melly May continued. "I did CPR like she'd taught me a few summers before. She choked up the water and started breathing but didn't regain consciousness." Melly May took a breath. "I would have kept her there until morning, but a huge storm came out of nowhere. I had to drag her into a cave, put a piece of my ripped t-shirt around her finger to keep it from bleeding, and tried with everything in me to keep her warm."

Lucy grabbed Melly May's hand. Melly May looked up at her with tears in her eyes.

"In the middle of the night, she stopped breathing. I tried CPR again, but it didn't work. Nothing did. She died in my arms taking part of me with her."

The room was silent. Tears fell down my cheeks.

"When did you decide to take on her persona?" Renée asked.

"In the cave that night," Melly May said. "I knew if I came back and went about my life, it might have taken days or weeks for someone to realize Misty was missing. But everyone would notice Melly May's—my—absence."

"That's not true," Lucy said. "At least, I hope it's not."

Melly May didn't reply to that. "What I didn't realize is how long it would take for someone to find her body."

"After a while, we had no choice but to halt the investigation," Jake said.

Melly May nodded. "I'd failed her so many times in life, then I couldn't keep her alive, and I failed her in death. Misty would have been a brilliant police officer. I was barely keeping up. Jake only gave me the job because he took pity on me."

Jake didn't deny the allegation.

"So you were going to end it?" I asked.

"I visited the cave often," Melly May said. "Somehow, it felt like she was with me there. But I was so tired of being alone. The only person who knew me had made a promise to forget me."

"A magical promise?" Renée asked.

Melly May nodded. "He obliged right after he gave me Wix."

Wix looked up at her, and it almost seemed as if he smiled.

"I put the ring on the rock so those people would find it, and maybe the police would start looking for her again," Melly May said. "Then that guy killed his wife—which I saw him do, by the way—and the attention turned to him. As if maybe he killed both of them. I took his car and crashed it. I was drinking. It was stupid. But at that point, I didn't care. I went back later and tried to move her body closer—outside of the cave—like I should have done when she died. But it crumbled. Even if I'd have tried to put the pieces back together, they wouldn't have been right. Misty was the one who was good at school, not me."

Jake rubbed the back of his neck. "What about the

magic? Did you really think your magic might have killed her?"

She shook her head. "I made all that up. We didn't fight. I begged her to come down."

"The magical coroner will be here tomorrow to make certain," Jake said. "My brain is too tired right now to think of what we'll charge you with, but I have to take you back to the hospital."

"Unless you want Renée to . . ." Lucy raised her eyebrows up and down.

Melly May reached for her necklace. "I'd rather spend the night in the hospital in pain than in jail."

"Is that why you wouldn't let me see your necklace?" I asked.

She turned it over and showed me—M.M. was engraved on the back. "You would have instantly known who I was."

Wix whined a bit when we all stood.

"Do you mind taking care of Wix for me until I get out of jail?" Melly May asked me.

"As long as Wix doesn't tear up any more pillows," I said. "I'm sure we can arrange that."

Melly May bent down and kissed Wix on his nose. "Please be good for Ellie."

Wix laid his head on her shoulder, and she wrapped her arms around his neck.

There was no doubt in my mind he would be absolutely perfect for me.

I didn't even bother with the feathers when Wix and I got back to the house. I needed sleep.

I woke to the smell of coffee and a wet nose on my cheek.

"Good morning, Wix," I said, patting him on the head. "Is someone here?"

Wix barked so loud I thought my eardrums might explode.

"They must be friendly if they made coffee, and you're not down there with Penelope chasing them away."

Wix pulled at the comforter.

"Okay, okay," I said. "I'm getting up."

I pulled my straight white hair up into a ponytail and threw on a hoodie.

"Anyone here?" I called as I walked down the steps. I had to rub my eyes to make sure they weren't fooling me. My house was clean again. "Bernardo? Did you do this?"

"Psssh," Katie said from the kitchen. "A man could never make a house look this good."

I didn't dare tell her that Bernardo had with his magic. "You cleaned my house?"

"Renée called all of us last night and asked if we wanted to substitute our morning yoga for a bit of deep cleaning."

I came around the corner to find Nancy, Amy, Fran, Bonnie, Renée, Bathilda, and Lucy sitting and standing around my island drinking coffee.

Tears welled in my eyes. "You shouldn't have."

"You do so much for everyone else," Nancy said. "It's about time we did something for you."

Bonnie handed me a cup of coffee. "Now, tell us more about this Bernardo fellow."

We sat and gossiped a bit about Bernardo and the Misty slash Melly May situation.

"And you just left him here to go off and work on a case?" Amy asked. "How do you know he's not back in Argentina?"

"I suppose he probably would have texted me," I said, then realized I didn't have a clue where my phone was.

"But you probably don't have your phone," Fran said.

I grabbed my satchel off the counter and rummaged through. "It's right here." I pulled it out and showed them, only to realize I had seventeen missed text messages from various people.

"You really need to get better about that," Katie said. "Remember that time I thought you were dead?"

I'd never needed a cell phone before I moved to Cliff Haven. "I know, I'm sorry."

"Don't tell us, tell Bernardo," Renée said.

"I'm texting him back right now." His messages were

just telling me he was still in town and we could get together whenever.

"I don't think you need to text him," Lucy said.

"Why not?" I asked.

"Because he's at your front door," Lucy said.

I glanced over at the front door. The drapes were closed over the glass inlay and the glass on either side. "How do you—"

The doorbell rang.

Lucy shrugged, and the other women looked at her in awe. Apparently, she didn't mind everyone knowing she was a witch.

Wix charged at the door, barking as if he was going to save us from the big, evil, scary monster.

"Wix, that's enough," I said as I opened the door.

Bernardo and Xander stood staring at Wix.

"What did you call him?" Xander asked.

"Wix," I said, trying to pull him back by his collar. "Not like a candle. W-I-X."

"Right," Xander said, quickly glancing at Bernardo. "And where did he come from?"

"He's Melly May's dog," I said. "Well, she was Misty, but really she was Melly May, and would you just come in already?"

They both stepped forward into the house, and I closed the door behind them. Wix went to work, sniffing them up and down.

"He's really sweet," I said, heading back to the kitchen. "I'm watching him for a while until Melly May gets out of jail. Do you want some coffee?"

I turned to find Xander and Bernardo still at the front

door, whispering about something. Wix stared at them like they were crazy.

"I think you're freaking him out," I said. "What's with the secrets?"

Xander looked at me. "It's nothing."

"Coffee would be wonderful," Bernardo said.

They finally left their positions at the front door and walked past Wix, both of them keeping an eye on him.

"He won't bite you," I said. "Are you scared of dogs or something?"

Wix pushed himself between them and came to sit by me. I patted him on the head.

"Something like that," Bernardo said.

"Well, don't be," I said. "He's harmless. Unless you're a pillow. Then watch out."

"We can attest to that," Katie said, peeking out of the kitchen at us. "I think we must have cleaned up about a million feathers."

"Everyone, this is Bernardo," I said when they finally followed me into the kitchen. "Bernardo, this is everyone."

The ladies introduced themselves to him individually.

"Sorry I ditched you guys," I said. "I got caught up in the case."

"It's no big deal," Xander said. "I didn't mind spending some quality time with my cousin."

"I'm glad you and Laura patched things up," I said.

"You are?"

I shrugged. "I heard you were pretty broken up about it. I don't want my friends to be sad."

I could feel his gaze on me, but I couldn't look at him. If I did, he might see how I actually felt about it.

"Bernardo has to head to the airport," Xander said. "I figured I'd let you take him if you were around."

Disappointment sank in my chest. Bernardo was leaving already?

Bernardo held my hand all the way to the airport. We chatted about the case and what he would do when he got back to Argentina.

I parked in the short-term parking. We walked into the airport hand-in-hand so slowly we were almost moving backward.

"Any chance you have plans to visit Argentina?" Bernardo asked.

"I don't have anything on my calendar, but I might have to make some." I squeezed his hand. "What about you? Did you like Iowa enough to visit again?"

"It was fun," Bernardo said. "Though I would have liked a bit more time with you."

"Next time—if there is a next time—won't be so busy," I said. "I promise."

"Do not get me wrong," Bernardo said. "I am proud of you. You are an excellent detective."

"Nah." I laughed. "I'm simply a recreational therapist who finds dead bodies."

"And their killers," Xander said.

"Or the reason for their deaths," I said.

We walked through the sliding glass doors to the security line entrance.

Bernardo pulled me to him, the passion of his kiss curling my toes.

When we separated, a couple of people in the airport actually clapped. I might have been embarrassed, but I didn't care who watched. I only had a few more minutes with this man. If only I'd spent more time with him instead of chasing around leads when there was really no crime.

"Stop," Bernardo said. "I can tell your mind is moving too fast."

"I feel terrible I wasted the time I could have had with you."

"Time is never wasted," Bernardo said. "It is merely used in different ways."

I started to say something, but he put a finger to my lips to stop me.

"You are the first woman I have wanted to be with in years," he said. "But I can sense a hesitation in you, and I think it has to do with Xander."

I looked at the floor. I wouldn't lie and tell Bernardo I didn't have feelings for Xander at all.

"Xander is a good warlock," Bernardo said. "But the two of you should not be together."

"Then it's a good thing we're not," I said with a laugh.

"But if things do not work out with him and Laura or you and me, you still should not be together."

"Why not?"

"That is not for me to say. And you may take this as my silly attempt to keep you away from him when I cannot be here to distract you, but it is not. I care for you and want you to be happy, whether that is with me or someone else."

My emotions showed in my hair. It changed to a shimmery copper color with little blue streaks.

"I do not mean to frustrate you," Bernardo said, cupping my face in his hands. "I like you a lot, Ellie."

I softened. "I like you too."

He kissed me one last time before walking away.

My lips tingled, wanting him to come back, but my head was filled with confusion. As I watched him disappear around a corner, I considered his words . . . and his kiss.

I didn't think men could be any more confusing.

Until I met warlocks.

***

Thank you so much for reading *Spelunking Speculation*!

Don't miss Ellie's next adventure *Festival Fiasco*!

Did you miss Ellie and Renée's vacation to Argentina? If so, pick up the FREE short story, *Argentina Abduction* right now at: **www.stellabixby.com/AA**

· · ·

If you enjoyed *Spelunking Speculation* and want to leave a review on Amazon or Goodreads, that would be amazing! Reviews help other readers choose which books to spend their time reading! You can also tell your friends about it too!

Also, I love hearing from readers! Email me at stellabixbyauthor@gmail.com.

XOXO,

Stella Bixby

ACKNOWLEDGMENTS

My biggest thanks has to go to my daughters who have consistently babysat their little brothers (for pay) this summer. Without them, I'd have never reached my goals.

Thank you, Nolan, for always supporting me, loving me, and encouraging me. I am so thankful for you.

Thank you to my friends and family for reading my books, liking my posts, and laughing at my stories.

Thank you to all of my readers who email, comment, and message letting me know you enjoy my books.

Thank you to my absolute rockstar beta readers. Holy moly, you guys know how to keep up! Your input is so crucial for these books!

Thank you to my ARC team, as always. Reviews are one of the easiest (and cheapest) ways to help authors!

And last, but never least, thank You, God. Your love in my heart makes me want to spread joy through my words.

ABOUT THE AUTHOR

Stella Bixby is a native Coloradan who loves to snowboard, pluck at the guitar, and play board games with her family. She was once a volunteer firefighter and a park ranger, but now spends most of her time making up stories and trying to figure out what to cook for dinner.

Connect with Stella on Facebook, TikTok, and Instagram.

Stella loves to hear from her readers!
www.stellabixby.com